CU00762044

LISA PIKE (Windsor, 1969) holds a PhD in Comparative Literature from the University of Toronto. Her fiction, poetry, and collaborative translations have been published in various anthologies and journals including *Re: Generations: Canadian Women Poets in Conversation*, *Columbia Journal*, *CV2* and *VIA: Voices in Italian Americana*. She is the author of the novel *My Grandmother's Pill* (Guernica Editions) and the poetry chapbook *Policeman's Alley*. Most recently, her collaborative translation with Anna Chiafele of Silvana La Spina's *Penelope* (Bordighera Press) received the American Literary Translator's Association 2022 Italian Prose in Translation Award.

Industrial Roots

Lisa Pike

HÉ/OÏSE

PRESS

Héloïse Press Ltd
4 Pretoria Road
Canterbury CT1 1QL

© Lisa Pike 2023

First published under the original English language in Great Britain by Héloïse
Press Ltd 2023

Cover design by Laura Kloos
Edited by Emily Riches
Text design and typesetting by Tetragon, London
Printed and bound in Great Britain by CPI Group (UK) Ltd, Croydon, CR0 4YY

The moral right of Lisa Pike to be identified as the author of this work has been
asserted in accordance with the Copyright, Designs and Patents Act 1988.

Every effort has been made to identify copyright holders and obtain their
permission for the use of copyright material. Notification of any additions
or corrections that should be incorporated in future reprints or editions of
this book would be greatly appreciated.

All rights reserved. Except as otherwise permitted under current legislation,
no part of this publication may be reproduced or transmitted in any form or
by any means, electronic or mechanical, including photocopy, recording, or
any information storage and retrieval system, without permission in writing
from the publisher.

ISBN 978-1-7397515-4-8

This book is a work of fiction. Any resemblance to names, characters,
organisations, places and events is entirely coincidental.

'I could just remember how my father
used to say that the reason for living was
to get ready to stay dead a long time.'

WILLIAM FAULKNER,
As I Lay Dying

CONTENTS

This book is for Len.

HIS LITTLE DOUCHEBAG

EVERY FRIDAY NIGHT there'd be a fight. He'd have his little douchebag – that's what I called it – sitting right beside the front door. In it he'd have a pair a clean socks, underwear, a change a clothes all ready to go. You wouldn't see him till Monday evening after work. Went straight on Monday from wherever he was. I don't know how many years it went on like that. Me, I never run around once – and I was pretty too.

That last time though, he got his. I was waiting at home with a Coke bottle. One a those real heavy glass kind they used to have years back. I was just sitting there by the front door in the living room, waiting to let him have it. I was gonna hit him smack over the head when he walked in. Never know what hit him.

It was the time a year of the Foreman's Dinner. They had one every year at Windsor Packers where Wally worked, though I never went. But for some reason that year, he asked me. I think it was one a those periods when we were on, whatchyamightcall, more friendly terms. So I said, sure, I'd go with him. I remember I got myself a nice dress too on sale, picked out my earrings and shoes, had everything waiting on the bed for me when I came home from work so I could change and get ready in a hurry. Wally was supposed to pick me up after my shift, we'd drive home so I could change and then off we'd go to the Foreman's Ball.

Well, my shift ends and no Wally. So I go upstairs to the office and call home. John answered and I said, 'is your dad there, hon? Let me speak to him.' But John said, 'no Mom, Dad left. He's gone to the Foreman's Dinner.'

'What!?' I said. 'Are you sure? What was he wearing?'

'His suit and tie.'

'Well, did he say he was coming to get me first?'

'No. He said he was going to the dinner.'

Well, I thought, that son of a bitch! And I had about five bags a groceries to boot! There was no way I could carry them all home on the bus! Luckily, one a the other cashiers said she'd drive me home; she was just getting off work too, so it was no problem for her and lucky for me or some a the food woulda got spoiled.

So I put the groceries all away, it was about 6:30 p.m. by that time, and went into the bedroom where all my clothes were laid out there, that dress so pretty that I bought, a real nice light blue that looked so good on me when I was young, and I thought: that's it, I'm gonna kill him. And I meant it too. One or two good cracks over the back a the head with that Coke bottle and he'd be out for sure.

So I waited. That was a Friday night and he came home on the Sunday. I kept checking the window every so often to see if I could see him coming up the road in the car. Well

I'd opened up the front curtains just as he was getting outta the car, and I could see that his clothes were all ripped up, the right sleeve of his jacket almost off and his white shirt all dirty and the cuts on his face. He came through the front door and instead a smackin' him over the head, I put the Coke bottle down and picked up the stick. We had one a those plants in the living room then that grows real tall and there was a stick in there that I put in to support it. A nice thick wood stick so the plant wouldn't fall down. I took it outta the plant and said, 'Wally, I was gonna get you with that Coke bottle over there but I see somebody already worked you over, I see somebody beat me to it.' He couldn't see the stick yet, I had it real close down beside my leg. He was still drunk and started heading to the bed without saying anything, just kinda stumbling his way in. And it was then that I let him have it. I hit him about three times across the back of his shoulders before he finally fell on his knees. But I didn't stop. And every time he put his hands up, you know, in front a his face to kind a shield himself, well, I just whacked those hands as hard as I could. And he'd put 'em up again and I'd hit him back down. He was too drunk to defend himself.

And then, the next day, not a word. He sat in the kitchen and ate breakfast like nothing happened.

But that wasn't the end of it. It was just the beginning, really. That next Saturday I went to have my hair done. I used to go down on Tecumseh Road there to have my perms when I could afford it, but mostly I went to have my hair set. So I was there with the girl doing my hair and someone says to someone else, some other lady in the chair next to mine, did you hear about the big fight last week at the Foreman's Dinner? And this lady, the one beside me said no, she didn't. Then they asked me if I knew about it and I said, of course, no I did not.

So this woman proceeds to tell everyone in the shop about what happened down at the hall where they had the dinner. One a the foremen started a fight and got tore up pretty bad. A course I knew they had to be talking about Wally so I just sat there quiet and listened. This woman proceeded to say that the fight was over a woman. That this woman was there with someone but that she was supposed to be the date of this foreman who ended up getting beat up. This foreman, everyone knew, also had a wife.

'Oh really?' I said, just to add into the conversation and let on like I wasn't the wife they were talking about. 'How interesting!' I said, even though I was madder than a hatter inside and had to keep myself glued to that chair to stop me from tearing outta that place immediately. 'So, what happened?'

'Well, apparently there was a big fight over this woman and the funny thing is, she isn't even pretty.'

'You don't say! You wouldn't happen to know her name, would you?'

'Sure, it's Gladys, she works down at the plant too.'

Well by this time I was just seeing red, but I didn't let on that I was upset. Just sat there like I usually do till my hair was set, gave my usual tip and then left. I wanted to see this cow for myself. See what I had been stood up for! So I drove down there, went inside and asked one a the guys if Gladys was working. They pointed her out to me across that huge room and I thought, well that son of a bitch! Standing me up for that piece a shit! One a the guys said, 'hey Ruby, you want us to call her over so you can talk to her?' And I said, 'No way! I've seen all I need to see here thank you very much.' I got in my car, drove straight home and made up my mind that I wasn't letting him in. If he was comin' in that house it would be over my dead body. I packed his little douchebag and put it on the porch and locked all the doors, closed all the windows tight.

He yelled and hollered out there for a while but eventually he took his little bag and he left. He stayed away for a while too. But eventually I guess he got his nerve back up and wanted to come home. It was John who told me. Said he saw his dad down at the bar and that he said he was coming home whether I liked it or not. And I said, 'he's crazy if he thinks he's getting in here.'

'Well,' John says, 'he's comin' home Ma.' So that's when I called Carl. Told him that his dad thought he was coming back here to live. 'I'll handle it, Mom. I'll be right over,' he says. And he was. Needless to say, Wally did not get in that front door. Try as he might. He finally drove away in a cab with that little douchebag of his. Little did we know he'd mortgaged the house to pay off his gambling debts. And more sooner than not, we'd all be driving away with our things too.

TWO-BIT TOMMY

'TOM'S GONE. The freight train got 'im.'

'*What?*'

'Yep, Linda called me this morning. He went to the store and he never came back.'

'But what are you saying? *You mean Uncle Tom's dead?*'

'Hit by a freight train. Poor Tommy. My brother Tom's gone.'

That was the way Gramma Ruby always talked. As if things just happened out of the blue and there was nothing you could do. Her mother got pneumonia and died (years later, I learned that the reason she caught pneumonia was because her second husband locked her out of the house in 50-below Winnipeg weather when she refused to hand over her old-age cheques to him); her brother John was taken over by his enlarged heart; Edward the youngest, had something that made his stomach swell up and he died (I can still hear him cryin' poor thing, I carried and carried him, my mother was desperate but the nearest town was fifty miles away); Auntie Stella (Mokriski, on the mother's side) died of diabetes but not before they had to amputate both legs, and her husband Uncle Walter (he used to be such a tall man!) ended up all shrunken and shrivelled in a nursing home so bad we couldn't even believe it, my sister Wanda and I, when we went back to Selkirk to visit. And so on. So many people with many ailments and deaths: why should Uncle Tom's be any different? A minor skirmish with fate where the freight train won. What was so unusual about that?

'Linda didn't say nothin' about the body though, whether there were parts missin' or not. I bet she don't know the full of it yet. They just told her he was in the car and for some reason he didn't stop. It was one a those crossings with no wigwam, just the flashing light or maybe even a sign I think. *I been killed almost twice by those myself!*'

Over the phone, I hear Gramma Ruby searching for her cigarettes followed by the sounds of her lighting up.

'She said he didn't want no big funeral. Good thing too 'cause I don't have the money to fly out there, though I'd like to be there for her. Elsie not dead a year, and now Tom. Linda's an orphan now, just like you. No parents a t'all,' she adds before finally taking her second drag. 'Wanda said we should go all in on the flowers but I don't even know where'd to send it. She didn't give me the address for the funeral, maybe we should just send 'em out to the house, but if no one's there? *What then?* They'll just go to waste. And do you think they'll even get there in time? Guess it depends when Linda decides to have the service, I guess. The police wanna do an autopsy before that.'

Gramma Ruby doesn't say anything more, though we are both there together, deep in the pause, her cigarette resting half on the edge of the round old-fashioned ashtray made of heavy amber glass with spaces enough for six burning cigarettes and twenty or so snuffed-out butts. It is the pause of the almost-said, signalled by her exhale of smoke, long and slow. Why, for instance, Wanda's suddenly so insistent on not only sending flowers, but being the one in charge, to do it, choose them, send them as if it were all her idea: the big fancy arrangement with the words '*Dearest Brother*' written on a sash of silk at the bottom. 'When I told her Elsie was dyin' a cancer and had maybe three or four days left to live, all she said was "oh well, that's no great loss." And I said, "Wanda! You should call Tom. He's your brother! This is for the living now! To make him feel a little better." And she said, "why are you so interested all a the sudden! After how Elsie treated Mother and Tom not lifting a finger to call us all those years like he didn't belong to us no more, cutting himself off from the family! Why are you so interested in corresponding?" "What she done to Mother wasn't right but Tom's your brother and he's reaching out now. *What matters is now, Wanda! It's not too late!*"'

This is part of what was in the pause, that in a time not too long ago – less than a year to be exact – Wanda had said who cares if Elsie is dying a horrible agonising death in the hospital from cancer, pretty much, she deserved it! And Tom, he kinda deserved the pain of it too, since he married her and allowed her to mistreat their own mother.

The other part of the pause, held tenuously on my end of the line, had to do with Wanda and Elsie, when a few years previous to Elsie's illness I'd gone to visit a friend after my own mother's unexpected death. Uncle Tom was part of the mythical landscape of the past, a life lived somewhere else among the people Gramma Ruby sometimes described. Aunties and great-uncles and cousins, each branch of the family having at least two or three Stellas, Walters and Wandas among them, so it took an effort for the listener to keep them all straight. If you didn't keep them all straight, you risked Gramma Ruby stopping abruptly, frowning deeply, and looking at you like you just weren't smart enough to follow a simple little story.

'*And this*,' she'd finally say, when I'd prompt her to get out some of her pictures ('at least to show the kids!' I'd insist, pointing to my own) 'is my youngest brother, *Tommy*!' The picture old and frayed, creased in places and slightly out of focus. A young boy of about nine or ten, standing up straight as someone's told him, with both hands at his side. He's not exactly smiling, but is appropriately serious for the serious business of taking a photo that it was in the late 1930s, early 1940s. The background of the photo is the same as many of Gramma Ruby's other pictures – a grassy field. In this picture, the chair present in some of the others, representing some sort of civilizing presence, is absent. And it is only upon looking very closely that you notice the holes in Tommy's striped T-shirt tucked into the pants clearly too large for him, pulled up tight round the waist with a worn dark leather belt. 'Yep! He was the youngest of all of us, except of course for

Edward. Edward never made it past being a baby. Only nine months old.' Who wouldn't want to visit Tom! See him there in the flesh and blood living all these years just outside of Winnipeg where my friend now was teaching. How would you not be able to look Uncle Tom up?

His voice was kind of timid there on the other end of the line as I stood at my friend's kitchen counter trying to have an inconspicuous conversation on a phone with a cord in a high-traffic zone. 'Hi, Uncle Tom, it's Lucy, your sister Ruby's granddaughter calling.'

'Yes,' he'd said, waiting.

'I know we've never met but I'm here in Winnipeg visiting a friend and I was wondering if you might want to meet me for a coffee?' Another pause, followed by the timidness opening up a bit into a kind of expansiveness tinged with relief. 'Oh good, I thought you were gonna give me some bad news about my sister. She's allright then? My sister Ruby?'

I say yes, because at the time she is doing relatively fine.

'And what about the other one? My other sister, Wanda? Is she doing allright too?'

'Yes,' I say, 'Aunt Wanda is fine.' The cord of the phone stretches around piles of books and bills awkwardly. 'Well I'll be here into next week,' I say, 'maybe I could take a bus out to somewhere near your place? Maybe there's a coffee shop or something out there?'

'Well, I got a guy coming on Monday to fix the tractor so I can't come then. But maybe we can meet some other day. If you call again after Monday then I can tell you when 'cause I'll know my tractor's fixed.'

'Okay Uncle Tom, I'll call you Tuesday then. Is the morning good?'

'*You saw my brother Tom?*' is what Wanda said to me over the phone when I got back. 'And did you tell him what I said Lucy? That message I told ya to tell him from me?' Her voice strident and militant, barely disguised and subdued by her present eighty-year-old physical state and body. 'Answer me, Lucy! I said: *did you deliver my message or not?*'

Equally important, however, was her need to have information about Uncle Tom's present looks. 'Is he skinny? Fat? Tell us!'

Gramma Ruby all the while smoking her cigarette while my great-aunt Wanda continued to interrogate me over Gramma Ruby's telephone. Finally, the conversation was taken out to the backyard on the cordless phone with Gramma Ruby tying up loose ends, going around dead-heading her roses while simultaneously saying, 'Wanda! Don't say that! Lucy's my granddaughter! I think we'd just better hang up before one of us says something the other one's not gonna like!' and with that, she threw the handful of dead rose blooms down in a particular patch of her garden along with a few snuffed-out butts she'd been carrying around in her cardigan and pant pocket.

This is what was in part of the pause: that Wanda's message went undelivered and that there had even been one in the first place. A nasty message to her youngest brother Tommy, even after all these years.

*

'Charles Street?' Tom had said. 'That's the name a the street where you live? My wife lived for years and years on Charles Street. Not yours a course. The one here, in Winnipeg, before we got married. Maybe I should take that as a sign,' he said, carefully watching me write down my address on the piece of paper that I'd folded around the copies of the photos I'd brought as an offering, a gift. 'Maybe I should take that as a sign that it's time to end all a that. *Yeah. Maybe it's come time afterall...*'

Gramma Ruby and I are still there together, complicit, neither one of us saying what's in the pause, neither one of us willing to articulate the unsaid.

'I'll call Linda tomorrow night to hear if she found out anything more. If she tells me where to send the flowers, I'll let you know. Other than that, honeybunch, not much is new. I walked up the street this morning to get my rat poison. They got me takin' so many pills now, I don't know what I'm on. Shoemakers and pill-pushers, all a them! You can bet they don't got to scrimp at the end a the month! Doctors and druggists, richer than all a the rest a us put together!'

She takes another drag in silence, a short exhale this time, unable to let it go. I see her in my mind's eye at the old dining room table made small for her apartment by removing what once was the permanent leaf. 'It wasn't three days ago that I was talking to him. I said, "Tommy, looks like me and you's in the exact same boat now. Both of us alone, with no one to talk to." Well, Linda was comin' out on the weekends, but during the week she had to work. Course, though, she'd leave Tommy the dogs. That's exactly what he was sayin' to me too. He said, "I got these damn dogs to feed!" I guess he had to cook up ten pounds a meat for them or something like that – that's how Linda keeps 'em, cooks for them and everything. And I said, "Tommy! At least they keep you company. I'm here holed up in this foxhole all day long, not a soul to talk to! You should consider those dogs good company!'"

'So tell me, how's everyone doing out east?' asks Uncle Tom, come to meet me in the airport the morning of my flight. 'My nephews? Tell me about my nephews.' Uncle Tom's metal-rim glasses reflect the fluorescent light at the ground level of the departure terminal. It isn't until we get up to leave the Tim Horton's though that we notice that right above us off to the side there is a restaurant where you can buy actual food.

'*Ahh!*' he says, 'now that's what I'd intended! To buy my niece breakfast. A proper thing with eggs and bacon and fried potato!'

I sit across from Uncle Tom thinking how he reminds me of Uncle Walter, one of my gramma's other brothers that I knew growing up. He had a bait shop and sometimes he'd let me come down to the basement to see the min- nows. I would stand up on a cement block to see them slitherswimming around in the vats, their tiny bodies all slick and silver, eyes looking round and wide, it seemed to me, at all the things around them: the vats, the walls, the ceiling, all made out of concrete and damp. Uncle Walter would skim some of the dead ones off the top, lit cigarette there between lips to the side of his mouth. When he'd removed sufficient numbers of the dead, he'd put the net down, take a thoughtful but not particularly long drag, and tell me to go on upstairs to the front part of the store and help myself to a bag of the pork rinds behind the counter. Uncle Tom, it was clear, would have been more handsome as a young man than his brother Walter. The sleeves of his pressed black shirt tucked into his jeans with the matching black leather belt are neatly rolled up on his forearms still toned and strong. 'And what about my sister's second husband? What was he like? Did he treat her allright? Cause you know the first one didn't. He was always mean to her. So, was he okay? He didn't hit her like the other one, did he?'

I reassure him that Gramma Ruby's second husband was fine before he finally died at the age of eighty-seven shortly after my mom passed away of cancer. Other deaths that I relate in some detail include that of the brother just a few years older than him, and my favourite: Uncle Mike. Cancer too, of the liver. 'Poor Uncle Mike,' I say, slightly surprised at how easy it is to slip into Gramma Ruby's ways: 'one morning he called up my gramma crying. "Sis," he said, "I need you to take me to the hospital! *Please Sis! Come right away, it hurts so bad!*" So she did. He died three days later. My mom and I went to see him the night he died. Didn't even tell anybody he had it. He didn't want anyone to have to worry for him.'

'Michael was a good man. After Mother's funeral he never took nothing. I asked him too. But he just shook his head, said no, there wasn't anything a Mother's he wanted to take. *All the others though!* They just swooped in: everything gone before I'd even known it!'

'He must a been scared though, maybe for one minute, when he saw it was gonna happen. When he saw it was gonna hit. Linda thinks it was his cataracts, that's why he didn't see it but I'm sure he could hear it comin', though I didn't say so to her. *My brother Tom wasn't deaf!* Must be terrible though for her. Imagine making dinner, someone going out to buy a little somethin', whatever's missin', and not coming back ever. She said she was waiting and waiting, checking out the window to see if he was driving up when the policemen knocked on the door. What a shock that musta been for her! Well, they musta been able to find a wallet or something on him if they came to the house,' Gramma Ruby half-concludes. 'Maybe it's like Linda said, now they're both together, Elsie and Tom. I know what that's like, living alone, and let me tell you, it's not fun! Now he doesn't have to feel lonely anymore, like me.' I hear her finishing off the cigarette in a kind of thoughtful silence tinged with anger at the edge.

'That was the life!' says Uncle Tom, his hands strong and warm as he looks through the small packet of photos I brought. Gramma Ruby had let me make copies of some of her pictures and I'd taken the liberty of making a few extras to give to Uncle Tom. The infamous picture of himself in his tattered clothes at age nine, a photo of a young Uncle Walter, maybe twenty-five or so with his mother when she came to Windsor to visit. Uncle Mike and his new bride Aunt Marian (*'Mother's face turned just ashen when she found out they were leaving Winnipeg for good to move to Windsor too!'*), and a group photo in the field with a number of Stellas, Wandas and Walters of several family branches and three different generations. 'I had the life a Tom Sawyer out there,' he said, going through them, firmly but carefully, one by one. 'All the fields and creeks out there. And my sisters, they'd get me to fetch the water. Wanda liked to have her baths and the water was half a mile away so I'd go get it for her. She'd give me two bits and I was happy for it – the movies were a nickel!'

I watch him from this side of the table, still sipping the large double-double he bought me and breaking off bite-size pieces of my blueberry muffin to eat. I can't see his eyes though; they remain there, hidden by the light reflecting off the lenses. (And this is the way they will remain in the picture I have a stranger take of us, arms wrapped around one another's backs with hands, fingers coming round firm to hold each other just below the shoulders, like good friends, sisters and brothers, *family*. It is just before my flight, just before Uncle Tom wheels the dark grey luggage, insisting on carrying my carry-on bag, the canvas strap securely over his left shoulder that he says: 'Remember to phone me when you get home! I wanna make sure my niece gets home *good and safe!*')

'*Oh there were so many a us at one time!* Six or seven people in the house. And if someone was visiting, maybe up to fifteen or twenty! And we'd make our own homebrew. Even after everyone'd left, all my brothers and sisters gone (*abandoning me to all the work!*) Mom and I would make our own. I had a still. You'd have a screen and ice on the top and we'd make twenty gallons which really was forty 'cause you'd have to dilute it. My mom worked hard. Back when I was a kid the women had all those heavy clothes to wash, underclothes. We collected rainwater for washing clothes and the water from the creek was good, *nice and soft.*'

I put another piece of the muffin in my mouth that I've already broken off to eat.

'I always had the idea to go back to Renwer to see what happened to Edward, my younger brother. There's probably some marker somewhere. He was sick and they put him in the wagon, it was fifty miles to the nearest town. He died on the way. I wanted to see if there's any church record or something, but I don't suppose I'll get up there now.'

'Wanda's got a mean streak, *you may's well know it!*' Gramma Ruby had said, going up the back steps after throwing down her butts and dead rose heads in the designated part of her garden patch. 'If she don't feel like she's got the upper hand, well, then there's trouble! That's why I said we'd just better end the conversation before it turns in the wrong direction. If you say somethin' she don't like, she might not talk to ya for a couple a years. And I don't know if I even got that many left!'

'But what did she say there, at the end, Gramma?'

'Better not say. You don't wanna know. I'm really mad at her, if you want to know the truth. And that's what I told her. Don't say that, Wanda! Lucy's my granddaughter!'

From the bits and pieces I could collect (if Gramma Ruby didn't barrel along with her stories about multiple persons with the same names encountering a variety of different or similar misfortunes, she threw out crumbs, sparse little bits and clips as she wished which sometimes did or did not make sense with what she'd previously said), my great-aunt Wanda saw her undelivered message not only as a particular instance of failure, but as yet another confirmation of my sad state of character and disobedience that went way back to when I was a small child and stayed with her sometimes over the weekend in Detroit ('when we picked you up this one time, she had you all dressed up in a miniskirt and little white go-go boots! Only you didn't want to go around with her so she could show you off to all her friends!' *or so the story goes...*)

'That Lucy never does follow through with anything! Not her marriage, not her job! Look at her now with this whole school thing, and to what good end? Tell me! Now this too! Not even enough courage in her to give Tommy my simple little message!'

'But what did Elsie ever do to her?'

'I'd already left Winnipeg to come to Windsor by the time my brother Tommy got married. They all lived together for a while. Wanda never liked her. One time Elsie burned a hole in Wanda's couch with a cigarette and then tried to cover it up. She's right about one thing though, Elsie didn't treat my mother well a t'all. There were many a Sunday Mother'd call me up crying, saying that she had no groceries in the house and Tommy was supposed to come by but didn't. And when we'd call Tom up about it, he'd say, 'Well, what do you want me to do? I got the meat shop to tend to!'

'*Hmm*.'

'Yeah, it was something like that.'

These are all the things caught between us, caught between me and Gramma Ruby. Bits and pieces and shards that we shift around in our conversations, sometimes stopping to examine them, sometimes not, depending on the mood. One thing we seem to agree upon though – we don't jostle things up too much. Someone could get hurt.

She tells me more about the soreness in her legs she's been having and how the doctors said her veins are collapsing ('it's not an emergency or anything though, so don't worry, it's not gonna happen tomorrow, but it is happening just to let you know. Honey! Your gramma's going down the tubes!') She tells me how she hates the new apartment she's in and having to live all alone, and how her sister Wanda's got it way better than her – only two kids she brought up and they treat her like a queen! 'Me, I raised five and look how they got me! I absolutely dread going downstairs to the garage to get the car, it's so dark I can barely see and then the bags a groceries are so heavy, everything's so heavy for me these days, and I look around and think, *Lord why am I here?* It shoulda been me Lucy, instead a your mother! All the other ladies at the grocery store still got their husbands to help 'em push the cart, not like me all alone. And those things too! They've gotten so heavy. *Did I tell you that I'm down now t'a just eighty-one pounds?'*

Uncle Tom touches my arm from across the table. 'Boy, you're hot!' he says, his hand firm on my forearm. 'Must be 'cause you're sittin' in the sun.' He puts the pictures inside the slip of paper with the address, my address 55 Charles Street, West Toronto, Ontario on it, and fits it all in the front of his shirt pocket. 'Well, I really appreciate having these. In fact, I'd wondered where'd my pictures went! I really missed having the one a me and my dad. Thank you, Lucy.'

'Did you know what Tommy was telling me that day too? He was telling me that Linda had been cleaning out some a the closets, getting rid of some a Elsie's things. And there in the bottom a one a them was a shoebox filled with all our letters – Wanda's and mine. Christmas cards and notes we'd sent him over the years. "Yep Sis, I've just been sittin' here reading some a them now," he said. Now why would she do that? Not only keep them from him, but hide them all in a shoebox for so many years?'

The sky is blue as Uncle Tom approaches the intersection. There are a few clouds there, white suspended. Linda has said they need eggs and fruit and milk for tomorrow's breakfast along with the Bisquick for her to finish making the cake from Elsie's recipe for dessert that night. The note is there, written and folded in his pocket, the pocket of his red plaid winter jacket with the Teamsters patch on it, which he touches. The freight train barrels along at high speed and he hears the long whistle, clear and loud, its loneliness drawn out. His eyes are fixed ahead on the road. His hands remain steady on the wheel and his foot is firm on the gas as if it's the most natural thing to do. His vision now the blue of the sky, the openness of the prairies, clouds slowly drifting into their own dissolution and letting go. The intersection like a doorway, simple and open which to pass through.

SKY BLUE

IT WASN'T UNTIL just after her fortieth year that she wanted to steal a baby. Marguerite had heard of this before. This kind of well-known lore, the kind of thing that floated in the air, no one questioning it or thinking twice. It was a well-known fact that women stole babies: it happened all the time. Middle-aged women or perhaps younger women who stole back the one they'd given up for adoption just before they'd changed their mind and now it was too late. But it was her own fault, people said, if she'd given it up. That's too bad, she should have known better and she'd certainly no right to it now. Why should she think that it would want to receive any of the videos she kept trying to send to the new parents? Mothers who give away their babies should just stop bothering people and leave well enough alone. They should just suffer and not think they can get away with kidnapping their own child back. Older women like herself – softer middle-aged bodies, stomach kind of doughy and pudgy in spite of the sit-ups and daily walks where they consciously tighten the abdomen to strengthen the core – could be seen in the mind's eye as bending in long dresses or skirts over baby carriages and prams, furtively looking up and around, seeing if there were a clear coast for their foibles. From where did we get such images? *Books? Newspapers? Films?* Then the little backstory would fill you in on how she didn't have any kids. Poor pitiful woman, desperate for children, understandable perhaps, but we still feel pleasure when she is punished. Send her soft slightly sagging body behind iron bars for a good long while. That'll teach her a lesson about the dangers of her infertility.

But Marguerite's situation wasn't any of these things. She was very fertile. She had three children with her ex-husband, all unplanned. The eldest borne of one single drunken night of not using any protection, the second a missed pill, and the third, well, the third was one single afternoon of sex slipped in between fights that were leading to the end of a bitterly failed marriage. Products of chance, happenstance, there they were: her children. No storybook romance or suburban fantasyland TV show life where grass is green with no weeds and granite countertops adorn fancy brushed steel double sinks with expensive multi-functional spraying faucets. Just the cold hard facts of life.

Marguerite had no reason to steal a baby. *I don't even want another baby!* she had finally decided, because now was the time to decide. She had another year, two tops, to have another kid. She'd thought about it long and hard. When she was turning thirty-eight, it still seemed like a real possibility. Years ago, she and her ex-husband had talked more than once about having a big family. Three kids for sure, but four didn't seem out of the question. Marguerite was thirty-five when the divorce became final. The ex was out, but that didn't mean there couldn't be somebody else. Even that marketing guy Bob she had dated for a while. He wasn't exactly father material, that she knew from the start, but she could raise it on her own. She knew how to do everything, and by now being by herself didn't scare her. In many ways it was better. Life was much easier this way. It was only the small matter of money that made you sometimes long for a partner. That, and the occasional remembering of a man's body hard and warm next to yours in the dark middle of the night.

But when thirty-nine and then finally forty came and she just hadn't had the will or desire to find someone new to date after Bob the marketer, she decided that it was done. Childbearing days were a thing of the past. She'd just have to get used to it. She was a middle-aged woman now and her children were teenagers. She'd have to adapt. Is this what it was then, this thing, this longing she felt lately whenever she was near a little chubby outstretched arm of a child, sweaty, barefoot in its stroller with toes pointing up? The knowledge, fear of slipping permanently away from the world of children, of babies? She still remembers that soft yet definite '*click*' shift of things when she was first let in. Proportions changed, everything now measured by the small baby's face. Her husband's head, for instance, suddenly became enormous, monstrous, its closeness to the baby's a clear desecration to the perfection she felt she, alone, had created. The child's flesh, bones, arms legs limbs, coming from her flesh, her blood, her effort. It was a world where the baby was the absolute centre, and she was unable to tear herself away, tenderly washing its body with gentle soft-smelling baby soap and dabbing at the remnants of the umbilical cord with a Q-tip dipped in rubbing alcohol like the nurse at the hospital had shown her.

Marguerite remembers that spring day, one of the first times she felt the pang to take one. She was walking with her eldest daughter on the street, small young trees flowering their pink and white blooms, the kind that people planted more for decoration than for any fruit they might bear. Her daughter was going to her singing lesson. Marguerite wanted to accompany her halfway, give her the cheque to pay the teacher, and then walk up to her favourite coffee shop to organize her agenda. They passed by a park. There were a number of children running around playing, dogs off their leashes chasing balls and sticks, adults clustered around, talking in between an intermittent throw, toss, push on the swing, nothing unusual. It was the child in the baby swing though, that made her feel the pang. A small baby smiling, laughing, arms and legs outstretched and open, body free and complete in the simple single action of being lifted up and down, carried effortlessly by the motion of its own weight. Marguerite could feel something twist around inside her, grab her from the inside out and squeeze around both sides of her ribcage. It was so sudden and intense this feeling, coming up inside her in such a painful and exquisite kind of way that it could have carried her over to the swing set not a hundred feet in the distance to snatch up the baby and run as fast as she could away, no plan, no destination; the important thing was to have the creature.

Or the baby in the train station. Marguerite there waiting with her book bag full of papers for work, looking up at the screen, waiting for the platform of her destination to pop up, her commuter ticket ready to be punched in at the self-service machine. The baby was a boy, maybe eight months, sitting squarely and messily in the seat of his combination baby-buggy pushchair playing with two ten-ride tickets. His older sister, a little girl of about four or five, came over to take them away, and knowing he'd cry, gave him a hat to play with as if that were a fair exchange. He whined and cried anyway but the mother remained unaware as to what had happened. Fussing, scrunching up his little face and then smiling when his sister gave the tickets back. So happy and satisfied, outstretching his sweaty dirty little arm to show his mother the prize, flesh so white soft and tender you'd want to take it in your mouth, kiss it or bite it. Marguerite all the while inching her way closer to the combination pushchair-buggy with the bustle of the train station abuzz, hum around her. *Children got lost all the time in places like this, didn't they?*

Before they were married and were young and still dating, Marguerite remembers her husband pointing out a small child of five or six, a girl in a Sunday dress with carefully braided pigtails walking along a fallen log. There was a group picnic going on in the park with families. She and Julian were out for a walk, holding hands, timidly treading what seemed to be the unknown path of the future. 'Do

35

you like kids?' he'd asked. 'Sure,' Marguerite had replied as if that solidified something about them, their relationship together as she eyed the little girl still walking with arms outstretched trying to hold her balance. Some adult called out to her in a language Marguerite didn't understand.

'Sure, I like kids,' Marguerite had elaborated, the little girl now running off to join the people who had called her as they were unpacking food onto a peeling green picnic table beside one of the small stationary public barbeques. It was true, but not fully. She did like kids but didn't ever really imagine having them. Marguerite's cousin Justine had just had a baby at nineteen, one year older than Marguerite was, and it really didn't look like much fun. Justine didn't look very happy despite all the fuss about the baby shower, presents, buggies, and little cute clothes so small they could fit a doll. It made Marguerite think of when she and Justine would play house in the basement.

Justine's dad had built her and her younger sister Kate a whole kitchen and laundry set out of real wood. There was a stove with burners and dials carefully and quite realistically painted on, a matching fridge ('without any magnets though 'cause it's wood but we can use Scotch tape to stick on this grocery list and a picture that Amy and Jack drew at school. KATE! Are you finished drawing the picture for us yet? We need it to put on the fridge. HURRY UP!'), cupboards filled with a variety of play boxes of cereal, plastic-pretend cans of soup, little pink dishes, plates bowls and cups, utensils in the little drawer that really pulled out by the sink. Our dolls looked at us from inside their strollers with the real straps so that they wouldn't fall out and get hurt: 'You don't want your baby to fall out and smack its head now do you?' Justine would say. 'KATE! Buckle her in tight!'

The sink was in the corner. It was what joined the appliances and the cupboard section together. It was like a real kitchen might be, only in miniature, and it was painted a pea-green that was so popular in kitchens of the mid to late 1970s. It was easy to imagine Uncle Will ('short for William, my mom doesn't like the name Bill,' Justine would sometimes explain to strangers) with his swatches of paint colour, holding them up, perhaps even testing some small samples on the back of the fridge or the stove to see how each would look. It was a real labour of love Aunt Kathy had said proudly and more than once that Christmas.

For Marguerite, it was a Christmas filled with absolute envy. A custom-built kitchen! Nothing could top that! 'Not that I had a chance anyway,' she half-pouted. Her own mother could only afford one Barbie and had said so long before the before-Christmas build-up of cheer-filled snowy expectation. It was easier visiting her mother's side of the family where everyone had nothing. Six girl cousins fighting over one small, coveted toy clothes iron. It also came with a miniature ironing board that folded up and had a flowered cover like a real one. But this wasn't what was attractive about it. After all, you could just as easily iron on the bed if you needed to.

The thing that made the ironing set desirable was the cord on the iron. It was a curly, tightly wound spiral that was somehow soft and hard at the same time as it looped two or three times around to lay on the ground before finishing gracefully into the magical object of everyone's desire: a small, grey cone-shaped suction cup that you could attach to the wall. '*Now you girls get away from here or you'll get your hands burned!*' Marguerite and some of the older cousins would say, menacingly holding the iron in mid-air.

The temperature of the iron could also be used in ways other than severe threats of mutilation; it could, for instance, be easily used to significantly prolong somebody's turn: 'These clothes aren't straight! It's still not hot enough! Can't you see all the wrinkles?!'

'Yeah,' another one of the cousins would chime in according to whatever alliances had been forming that particular day, 'she's not done yet! Her baby can't go out with wrinkled clothes!' Sometimes some of the smaller kids would think they were smart and sneak up close beside the wall – having gone both underneath the ironing board and in and among the legs of the people in play – to quietly unplug the cord, the idea being to put an end to someone's turn. Only this never happened. All their sneaky cleverness gone to waste as the older girl with the iron held in mid-air quickly snapped in fierceness and play exasperation: 'It wasn't even on! Now I have to start all over!'

Often enough, things could escalate. It could easily go from pulling the cord out from the wall and the imaginary electrical outlet to pulling on each other's clothes, hair, whatever could be found and held onto. A few of the cousins were quick and adept scratchers, seeking and grabbing onto flesh almost instinctively; Lucy was the only one who would consistently bite. She was still young enough to get away with it. Putting on her 'I'm still a little girl' face after the whole rough-and-tumble scuffufle was over, the ironing board still with its cheery domestic flower cover lying helpless and awkward on its side. '*Is it broken?*' they would all ask when they came to themselves and remembered the game, trying to recall at which point they were and whose turn it was next.

Marguerite's life was so incredibly incomparable to that of her cousins Justine and Kate. Uncle Will had money and was interested in actually being a dad whereas neither of these things were true for Marguerite's father, run off when she was just two weeks old, quitting whatever job he had so he wouldn't have to pay child support. Uncle Will tried to take on his brother's responsibility to Marguerite on top of the responsibility to his own kids as much as he could with weekend sleepovers and invitations to go on vacations Marguerite's mother couldn't afford.

On their vacations, sometimes all the way to Florida, Marguerite and Justine would share a bed and make Kate jealous by calling her a baby and elaborating on the pet name Aunt Kathy had for her youngest daughter: monkey. 'Monkey! Where's my little monkey?' they'd taunt in a high fake-lady voice that was supposed to be Aunt Kathy's. 'Come here, baby monkey, you're so jumpy and hairy! Arms hanging long and your little butt so white and flat! *Come to Mommy!*' Whatever came to mind about chimps and their various body parts and behaviours, Marguerite and Justine would say it to Kate till she streaked off crying to tell her mother – though only select bits so the girls wouldn't get her even worse, later.

Marguerite's husband Julian had liked to build things too. Apparently, according to the kids, he was still busily at it in the basement of his new house with his new wife. It was drywall he loved in particular. Tiling could be fun too, he'd said, after attending a workshop on it at the local hardware store. He tiled the floor of their small home office and had plans for the rest of the basement, a family room, just before the divorce. Marguerite got to choose the paint for the room: Sky Blue. She remembers sitting there at the new desk looking up off to the left out the small one-by-two foot window, the sill level with the ground, feeling only her feet freezing on the cream-coloured designer tile in spite of her thick socks. 'Wow!' everyone said when they came in for a tour of the house, 'you're so lucky your husband's handy!'

Julian would spend hours downstairs, measuring, bending, reaching, using a small rigid metal tool shaped like a corner along with a level with yellow bubbles to get all the various lines and angles straight. Well into the night he'd be there, cleaning, leaving everything just so, ready for the next day when he got home from work. Sometimes during the summers he'd be working on an outdoor project and they could all be closer together, there in the yard. The kids playing in the sprinkler or the blow-up pool while he raised flower beds, built a shed after laying himself the concrete foundation into which he wrote their children's names with a stick. 'There's lots of room to store their outdoor toys in here too!' he'd said, smiling, readjusting the lawnmower and the new weed-wacker to gain the most efficient use of space. The kids running around squealing, the spray of water rising high up in the air, one of them having detached the dark green hose from the sprinkler to make a rainbow, fine mist catching the sun. *We almost seemed like a family*.

When the doctor told Julian that he couldn't tell him anything about Marguerite, about the things she'd said and told him, he looked like he might cry. Marguerite had never seen Julian cry before. Only a little tear in his eye when his grandmother in Italy died. It was to be expected, he'd said, she was old; everyone had to die sometime, he'd half-smiled scooping the car keys up off the kitchen island on his way out the front door to buy the wood for the new deck. Julian's face, so surprised by the young doctor's firmness, resoluteness, insistence on doctor–patient confidentiality, touched her in some way. His soft green eyes, the hand that held hers and almost twenty years of their life together there on the white hospital sheet of the bed. Marguerite tried to say something as he got up but it remained just with her, trapped inside her head, her mouth and mind having been disconnected years ago, one from the other.

The young doctor's voice was soothing, though he seemed to get emotional too at a certain point, telling Marguerite that his mother was sick too, and one time she had to go away on a plane somewhere. 'We didn't want her to go,' he said, as if this whole story was to explain something about Marguerite and why she was in the hospital bed, 'but she was just too sad. She couldn't stay. And that's how life is,' he said, 'you're not guaranteed anything. Not even the love of your children when they grow up.' Marguerite didn't understand all of the doctor's story. It seemed like a few odd bits of something, string of different sizes, thread with knots, pieces of wool all clung together in a ball that needed to be sorted out, matched up.

Marguerite was grateful for the way the sheets felt stiff, tucked in all around her on the bed. The air smelled and sounded of women-bustle, disinfectant and medicines. *Maybe now I will be safe.* She turned toward the wall and closed her eyes, the part about your children maybe not loving you when they grow up ringing in her head.

On one of their halfway walks, just as Marguerite was handing over the cheque for her daughter's voice lessons, Lucille said she had decided that she wanted to go and live with Julian. She didn't mind Mary, the new wife, like her brother and younger sister did and her dad's house was closer to the high school and her new job at the mall. 'Besides, I'm sick of going back and forth back and forth every week now, it's tiring! I just want to stay in one place. I'm not choosing him over you,' she said, dogs running, sticks being thrown in the background, 'I'm just making a choice for me. You can understand that, can't you, Mom?' Marguerite feels the pang coming up slow from inside her, its steady creep this time instead of something quick and hard, seizing. It wraps itself slow and stealthy, winding itself in and out of the openings of her ribcage until her breath is there, all caught up inside.

'Yes, I do,' says Marguerite, feeling how the pang is there, wrapped around her insides, part of organs, bones, flesh. 'I do understand that.' She touches Lucille's face, brushes her hair back and looks into her eyes, the same colour as Julian's, and kisses her on the cheek. *Mouth, head, breath connect.*

'See you later, Mom!' Lucille waves, arm outstretched high above her head with the signed cheque. Marguerite watches her daughter walk the straight of the cement side-walk between the rows of decorative trees to her voice lessons teacher's house, a young woman in her twenties who has made a music studio out of her basement. The sky is blue as Lucille disappears, Marguerite standing alone now at the halfway point, the feel of her book bag resting there on her thigh. She turns, heading for her favourite coffee shop, a small piece of cord, the very end where it attaches, in her mind.

AT THE BOOTLEGGER'S

SOME WOMEN TOOK TO DRINKING themselves, you know, to cope. Thank God I never did. Only smoking. And that's exactly what did happen to Doris across the street in the house right opposite mine. I don't know how many times I'd seen her stumbling up the steps real late at night. Falling down too on the lawn. It was her daughter Patty who finally found her in the upstairs bedroom one afternoon after coming home from school. Coming home to find her mom like that, dead, finally OD'd. Yep. That's how some women ended up.

Alot coulda been done with those houses. Fix up the basement, have a rec room there, maybe another bedroom. But very few men had a mind to do that. You'd have to have an interest in the family. Nine outta ten didn't. Nine outta ten were only interested in their whisky and women. Three, sometimes four kids sleeping together in one room – it was tight living, that's for sure.

It was the house third from the corner on my side a the street where they used to bootleg. One time Wally took Peter in the car, drove around the block to end up right back there. It wasn't till I was sitting on the porch down the road at Marguerite's that I noticed the car. In fact, it was Marguerite who pointed it out. I went over to her place after Wally left and said, 'well, the old man's at it again. Took off. This time with Peter and I'm really worried.' It wasn't a few minutes later that Marguerite said, 'well Ruby, isn't that your car?'

So I marched right over there, opened the door and said, 'what are you people doing! Who gave him that beer? I wanna know, and I mean right now, which one a youse put that in his hand! You all know how many kids he got and with no monies to spare! You should all be ashamed of yourselves, doin' that to his kids!' And a course there were women there too. 'I'm calling the police!' I said. 'The minute I get home! You'll see how funny it is then when you all get a fine.' Which is exactly what happened. The cops came and fined 'em for bootlegging. Peter there, he was just little then. His dad bringing him to a place like that! I took him by the hand and said, 'honey, this isn't a place for you, you better come home with me.'

When the boys got bigger, that's when they started standin' up to him. One time, Wally and I were having it out about something in the living room and Peter came home after school. He came in and said to his dad, 'I'm sick and tired of listening to you call my mother those filthy names; I can hear you all the way coming up the street! Now this is gonna stop, like right now. And I mean *today*!'

Well, Wally gets up from where he was sitting and says, 'you little punk! Talk to me like that!' He was getting up, like to hit Peter, and Peter was gettin' ready to hit him too. So I went between them to stop him and said, 'Peter honey, don't let him suck you into doin' that.' 'Cause it says in the Bible that you're not supposed to raise your fist to your parents and there's that part, you know, about your hands dryin' up if you do and that kinda scared me.

So I said, 'honey, don't let him do that to you, make you feel guilty for the rest a your life for hittin' him. *You don't want'a live, with that on your shoulders.*'

ROSES OF SHARON

THE SHIT HAS ALREADY dried up on my mother's back. She sits squatting over the toilet with her summer jersey cotton nightgown pulled up, the bottom hem up on her knees held with her hands as her torso bends forward at the waist. She is not crying, just shaking a little. Like the cry isn't strong enough to muster itself up into existence, never mind let itself out. I take one of the baby wipes out of the package and clean her back. And though they're thicker than the normal baby wipes and made for adults, they still smell like and remind me of babies. I say something reassuring to her, something like, 'it's OK, don't worry, let go, it's fine,' all the while wiping the shit that has sprayed up from the diaper she was wearing away. One, two, three dirty baby wipes lying on the corner of the small bathroom sink; I'll disinfect everything later. 'Yeah,' she says, her voice a thin strand, 'maybe that's what I should do, *let go*.'

Her husband comes in the door only to turn up his nose before walking away. I tell him I'll take care of things as he shuts the door on us both; I continue to wipe until her back is clean. She tells me she can do the rest, that she'll clean herself underneath with the wipes, and that Tammy's coming at 1 p.m. to give her a bath. I don't have the heart to tell her that for whatever administrative reason the home-care worker's been changed again and Tammy won't be coming back after today. Let that be one of this afternoon's crises and disappointments; I can't deal with it right now.

'*Don't worry Lucy*, I have to deal with these professionals. You have your own things to do at home. Besides, Gary doesn't want you here, he says having people around doing things for me makes me weak. And right now, I gotta be strong if I'm gonna beat this thing.' That's what she said when they'd sent her home the first time. I'd wanted to tell her that I didn't give a flying fuck about Gary and what he wants but I didn't want to set her off crying again, pleading for everyone to just stop fighting. 'I don't want to hear anymore!' she'd cry. 'I just can't take anymore of everybody always arguing!'

It was about the laundry basket, a tall wicker basket beside my mom's bed that she used for dirty clothes. I'd moved it, along with some other pieces of furniture on the path from the bathroom to the bedroom so that she'd have an easier time with her new walker. When I came back from the pharmacy with more diapers, wipes, foaming hand disinfectant and wash, a special sip cup, plate and spoon along with the container for the disposal of used syringes, he'd moved everything back to where it had originally been. 'Gary!' I'd shouted. 'She needs the path clear. How can she even get out of the bedroom with that huge hamper blocking the way? And the same thing needs to be done so she can get out the back door. She can't even get out to the back porch for some sun if she wants to. That's what I'm doing this afternoon. I'm going to move that table and all those plants so she can get through with her walker.'

'No, you're not!' he'd shouted back, his six-foot-four frame towering over everything. I hadn't noticed before how much weight he'd put on over these past few years. Suddenly he seemed to me to take up the entire room. 'You're not gonna be changing a goddamn thing in here Lucy! Everything is going to stay exactly the same. Exactly where it is! She's the one who's gonna have to adjust. And if things are difficult for her, all the better! It means she'll just have to fight harder!'

'That's ridiculous! We have to make things easier for her so that she can concentrate on getting better! Everything in here can't stay the same!'

'And that's exactly why you're going home the day after tomorrow. You're making her weak, giving in to her every little whim. She needs to be strong and fight and this is how she's gonna do it!' Both of us stand just inches from the laundry basket, ready to grab it as things begin to move over into the realm of physical violence despite the fact that he is two, three times my size. We are drawn back, made to slide out of it by my mother's whimpering cries from the couch. 'Just stop! Just stop!' she insists, breath all shaky and fragile as she reaches out to her walker.

'Mom. It's OK, it's fine, nobody's fighting. I'm going to go get the stuff I bought at the pharmacy. I'll wash the cup out so you can use it right away with your *Boost*.'

'What?' she says, her breath all held within as she tries to gather herself up. 'I thought I already took what I needed a that stuff today.'

'You need to drink two of those a day, *remember*?'

She moves back into the little-girl whimper again.

'But I don't want anymore a that,' the little girl says. 'It makes me feel sick.'

'The doctor says you have to. *'Member*? It's so you can put on weight.'

'Oh yeah. Right.'

Her little body sinks back into the couch.

The abandon comes when you're in the hospital for the third or fourth time and the one round of chemo has gone fine but you don't weigh enough for the second.

'Do you want to know what's going on Mom?' I ask, the two of us alone in one of the hospital rooms, she sitting in the visitor's chair behind the door that opens up into the hall.

'Do you want to know what happened in the surgery?'

'No,' she says, in some other voice I can't place.

'I'll tell you what's been going on and what's happening now.'

'No,' the voice repeats. 'I don't want to know.'

It is late afternoon, the crest of the day fallen, dull summer cloud cover hanging on outside the hospital window until the gradual approach of night.

'OK,' I say. 'I won't.'

*

When Gary is in his La-Z-Boy, whisky in hand and bottle on the table in front of the TV for the night, I move the wicker basket into the furthest corner of the room and crawl into bed with my mother. I haven't slept with her since I was a small child. And even then, doing so was rare. A teenage mom bouncing from job to job and boyfriend to boyfriend trying to figure out how to survive life on her own with child in tow.

'Do you forgive me for your childhood?' she'd said, the night before she went in for the operation.

'Yes,' I'd replied, hugging her, resentful. Manipulative to the end is what I'd thought in that moment, asking that question when she knows I won't say no.

'It's just that I'm so afraid. What if they open me up and I'm full of it? I always thought I'd be this little old lady with her herbs in her garden.'

Her body is warm; I adjust the extra mattress cover, the medium-sized one that fits under someone's bum in case there's a leak. Her breath is there beside me and on the other side of her body – now nearly half the size of what it normally should be – are the three pillows I placed length-wise so she won't fall off the side of the bed, its height specially matched to Gary's. It isn't until the very last that he gives in to the hospital bed brought in by hospice to be set up in the dining room right beside the bathroom. The act of packing it all up after she's gone is interspersed with him stepping out onto the front porch holding onto the metal railing with the black rusting paint to retch over the side. 'It's nothing. It's nothing,' he repeats when I come out

53

to see if he's OK. 'It's just my throat. It keeps constricting. I don't know why.' The sheets are the ones with the Roses of Sharon hand-embroidered along the edge. I pull them up over us both; she is asleep.

The morning light comes through the window, plain hospital curtains pulled back to expose the view of the street. I see and hear the cars pass; in one hand I hold the bag with the sip cup, in the other a tea from the cafeteria to feign normalcy. My mother sits up slightly from her inclined position on the bed while the nurse finishes washing her hair and then drying it with the inside of a baby's diaper.

'After she does that,' my mother says, little girl half-smiling, 'it's almost dry. That's how they do it here. *To everyone.*'

MOTHER'S BONES

THERE IS SOMETHING beside her bed with the bones of her mother in it. It is a container that her mother used for tea, to keep her teabags in. Some people in Maude's family think that's a personal touch, but Maude just thinks it's sick and that her mother would be appalled. She can just imagine her mother, sticking her hand in there to get one of the loose chamomile teabags, kettle boiling, steaming hot vapor rising up out the front, listening to the tail-end of someone suggest that after she died, her cremated remains would be put inside her tea container with the sprig of rosemary on the front under the actual words '*Rosemary*' written in fake handwriting on a cheesy angle. Anyone tries to do that to me, Maude, you'd better fuckin kill 'em.

Maude's family also thought nothing of the way her mother's second husband had delivered her ashes: in a shoebox with ADIDAS written on the side. And, because the tea container wasn't a proper urn that could be sealed, Gerald had wrapped a bunch of grey electrical tape around the top.

Four years later, Maude still gets the nauseous feeling rising up inside her with the sensation in her legs like they're two rubber bands that have been stretched too tight, and now they're all loose and wobbly and won't let her stand upright. Gerald had shoved the shoebox at her hard, almost pushing her right back inside Gramma Ruby's front door, the screen all hesitant on its hydraulic hinge before suddenly slamming shut tight. She stood there inside the front door with the mirror right beside the 'God's Prayer' plaque 'Thank God for Mothers' that the youngest uncle had given Gramma Ruby on one of her many Mother's Days, the fake plastic roses in a clear cut-crystal vase underneath it on the shelf, holding the ADIDAS shoebox while Gerald drove away in the minivan. No one thought that was strange. They just thought that Gerald was upset and should be forgiven. 'Being so angry all the time, Maude, is not good for your health,' one of the aunts would say. 'Call us when you feel better.'

But Maude never felt better. Now, after four full years (parts of which she sometimes makes an effort to remember, call up from amid the dark patches of blank she still has), she felt like she was finally coming to accept that her mother was dead, but she didn't feel 'whatchyamightcall,' as Gramma Ruby sometimes said in one of her mealy-mouthed ways, 'better.' She understood now, that her mother wasn't coming back. That she wasn't going to show up suddenly one day or come at the very last minute to one of the interminable, never-ending string of special occasions. Her birthday, her kids' birthdays, Christmas,

Hallowe'en (Cheryl's all-time favourite) or even the newly invented Family Day by the Conservative Party, who still held on increasingly desperately to their sad little minority government.

When Maude finally graduated from university she had waited around all day, especially during the ceremony before they read out her name, sure that her mother would show. After all, they'd been talking about this day for years. Cheryl and Maude were supposed to go on a special trip to celebrate, Maude the only one in the family ever to have graduated from university. But they couldn't go now because Cheryl was dead.

Even after the graduation, after Maude had been called up, her name read, no one there smiling, taking a picture or congratulating her, she just felt disappointed that Cheryl didn't show up. It didn't feel like Cheryl was dead forever, it was just like she didn't come but would be there for sure next time.

Gramma Ruby came with Aunt Stella and Gramma Ruby made a big deal about there being an empty chair beside them, 'that was for your mother' she said, 'I smelled her patchouli.' Maude was sick of Gramma Ruby going on about smelling her dead mother's patchouli in public places: Convocation Hall while the ex-first woman prime minister of Lithuania gave the graduation address, out for dinner eating pasta, in the car driving to get groceries. It was a bunch of bullshit. Her mother was dead and was never coming back, not to anyone's graduation, or dinner, or along for the ride on the way to Price Chopper. *Get that through your fucking head!* Maude wanted to shout. But you can't shout that out to a little old lady, it wouldn't be polite. So Maude just listens to all this bullshit. Meanwhile, the mother's ashes still remain in the tea container with the lid beside Maude's bed. She took the electrical tape off but keeps the whole thing in a small cupboard inside the nightstand – in part to avoid a spill, in part to keep the whole fucking mess out of her sight.

In her mind lately, Maude often sees the urn. Not the old urn from the funeral, which was pretty enough: teal blue marble, $500, she checked it online. Simple, elegant, her mother would have approved. It suited her. On the front there was no plaque though, with her name engraved. Just a sticker, clear so that you couldn't see it except for what was written on it in plain black lettering: first name, married name, and the dates 1947–2005, two years short of sixty. 'I always thought I'd be a little old lady working in my garden,' Cheryl had said one of those nights when they were sleeping together in the same room. A thought, a statement lucid and coherent plucked from all the hallucinations and screaming and general hysteria caused by her terror and fear. 'Now I have to say goodbye to my daughter,' was another.

Maude remembers when they called her to say her mother's kidneys were failing and the body was beginning to shut down. She remembers how she couldn't really take that news in. That particular call just like any other call from the hospital – her white blood cell count was low, the round of chemo went surprisingly well, all calls and updates to prepare her for the next time Maude came in to town. Her boss had called right after that. What was the call about? She doesn't remember, in fact, it seemed odd that she would be calling that time of day at home. Maude was literally on the way out the door to teach, a bundle of student essays to return to the class in hand. Judith, the college principal said, 'Oh my God Maude, you'd better go, you need to leave right now. Call a cab for the papers, have them delivered to me and I'll return them to students. Then you should get on the road, maybe you should take a train, I don't think you should be driving when you're this upset.'

But that was the thing. Maude wasn't upset. She wasn't anything. Her mother's kidneys were shutting down, that means one to three days at the most, but what did that really mean? The kidneys shutting down? When she got to the hospital, everyone focused on that. The kidneys shutting down. The rate at which that was progressing. Nurses, and then family members too, going over to the side of the bed to check the plastic bag that was hooked up to the catheter. 'Not much, a little, I don't know, it seems a little more full to me,' they'd say, flipping the bag over or even holding it up a little to better study the contents. If it were the nurse, something would get written down on the chart attached to an official-looking clipboard. And that's how it was with the kidneys.

On the third day, the kidneys shutting down became tinged with annoyance and impatience, though no one would ever say it. The checking of the bag lost its novelty and the morbid curiosity of seeing someone's innards flow-ing out of them, the last trickle of bodily fluids drain, just wasn't as interesting as it was on day one when the news had been announced. The nurses came in just the same and jotted things on their clipboard, but there just wasn't the same air of 'oh, here we go! it's begun,' somehow friendly and sociable mixed with sympathetic chatter. Instead, it was filled with a kind of grey 'when is this going to be over?' air accompanied by the bland scratching of pen over paper. The heart didn't really seem to be weakening either. In fact, it was almost as if Cheryl was refusing this 1–3 day medical fact of the kidneys shutting down. 'Rarely, *rarely*,' said the nurse, 'does this go to the third day. The norm really is 1–2. Was your mother a walker? *Runner?*' Three days and there she was, somehow still alive.

The urn that Maude sees in her mind is the one she's supposed to get, be responsible for now that Gerald (to whom her mother left every goddamn thing – her half of the house on Aubin Road, any assets, monies, and the trailer out by Ridgetown) had smashed the original blue teal one with a fucking hammer. 'That's what she wanted,' he kept repeating to everyone in between a swig of beer and the other bullshit he was spewing on any particular given day. 'She wanted it to be a private thing, between me and her, spreading her ashes out on the beach by the Rondeau marsh.' *T h e R o n d e a u f u c k i n g m a r s h*. Smashing open the urn with a hammer. Sticking his grubby hand in there to scoop out what he considered to be his half, and then dumping the rest into her tea container to wrap up with electrical tape and put in an ADIDAS shoe-box to give to Maude. And silence on this from everyone. Uncles, big dangerous uncles who as a kid Maude had seen do all kinds of violent things for much much less – hard backhands for talking too loud, open-palmed cuffs on the back of the head for talking back, coming over with two-by-fours to beat the shit out of one of Maude's mother's boyfriends. But that was back in the day. Now they were all mealy-mouthed pricks living in places like Calgary and Scarborough. So it's up to Maude, they all say (without talking to her directly of course), to get the new urn and make things right.

Gramma Ruby too, in her day so formidable, ruling for so many years the street nicknamed Policeman's Alley in the neighbourhood with all the cheap housing built for returning World War II vets in behind the old Ford's Test Track. Not taking shit from the men or the police who came to arrest them. '*Well, they didn't call it Policeman's Alley for nothin!*' she would still sometimes say. Even she was powerless in the face of this. She had tried, however, pulling one of her old tactics out for the occasion. 'Sometimes you gotta be nice,' she'd said to Maude, 'to get what you want.' The end justifies the means. In fact, she'd gone all out. Cooked up a big dinner, brought up cold beer from the basement fridge and watched while her son-in-law ate for the most opportune time to talk to him about her daughter's ashes, about blessing them and then spreading them, as a family, all together. Only it was too late, he'd already done everything without telling anyone. It was the next morning that he'd wheeled up in the Chrysler minivan with the shoebox to give to Maude. Gramma Ruby had tried, you have to give her that, and she was a little old woman now of eighty-six.

Maude remembers her mother being so alert those days just before she lost consciousness and the kidneys had started to fail. She almost seemed like her old self and like, somehow, odds against all odds, she was actually going to get better. Cheryl was even sitting up in bed eating. She'd asked that the curtains be opened up so she could see outside while she ate her soup. 'Ah, Tecumseh Road,' she'd said, sitting there actually spooning some of the soup into her mouth herself. Chicken noodle. Maude was thanking her for all the phone calls, saying how she really couldn't have finished her university degree without them. Cheryl sat up in the bed even further to say with great intent and purpose: 'Whatever it takes!'

Trying to complete her degree after the divorce, living in another city, cut loose from everything that had been her life, sometimes going to the therapist's in her pyjamas, Maude had been living off vitamin drinks and Lorazepam (and cheap beer and wine before she finally kicked that sorry-assed Seamus out). Cheryl would call her in the morning before she left for work, tell her it was time to get up, just like when she was a little girl and would wake her up for school. Then, she would call at around 10 a.m. on her break from her cell phone, and of course at lunch. Then the series of afternoon and evening calls once she got home from work. When Cheryl got sick but Maude didn't know yet (no one but Gerald knew), Cheryl hadn't called Maude for a week. 'How does that feel?' asked the therapist.

'Well, it's unheard of. It's never happened before. A week! May as well be a year. My mother never ever does that!'

'OK, *but how does that feel?*' the therapist repeated, always trying to get Maude back to thinking about how she felt, what were the emotions you could feel about things.

'Well,' Maude paused, 'I think it feels great!'

Cheryl didn't call Maude because she had cancer and was in shock. But it was also embarrassment too. 'Everyone at work is going to know,' she said to Maude later, 'they're going to say: "*See! And she was such a health nut! Just goes to show you!*"' as if getting cancer were her fault, punishment for thinking she was so great, eating healthy and exercising and all.

The urn is teal, like the last one, but it has other colours too: jade green, yellow and a kind of purple that turns into mahogany as it takes the forms of branches and leaves. Its shape is slender, elegantly rising to the top, the place where it will be permanently sealed. Is this what prevents Maude from clicking on 'order here'? Maude still unwilling, still railing about everyone's failings, still seeing her aunt (the one whose husband had recently been forgiven for winding up high in bed with a hooker even though he was much too old now to be excused for such shenanigans!) standing beside Gramma Ruby's old wooden kitchen table where the ashes had first been placed, reaching in to actually touch some of them and picking up a shard of Maude's mother's bones, rubbing and rubbing it between thumb and forefinger – like some kind of talisman.

COWBOY KENNY

THE PARKING LOT begins to fill. The sun is high overhead as people get out of their cars; older ladies are given a hand, lifted gently but firmly up out of the seats they'd settled into for the long ride. Their men are of the age of those who still like to wear light-coloured patent dress shoes without the laces from the 1970s, a small piece of chain or strap going across the front. Some part of the outfit is also in polyester, though not the pants – their waists having grown too much in girth since then. Only a remnant or two remains now of what had originally been designated the 'funeral outfit' at a time in their lives when the people they knew had started to die.

A mother. That was the hardest. A good brutal initiation into the concept of mortality. A great-aunt (old, under-standable), an uncle (failed triple bypass, died on the table, regrettable since he was still a young sixty-one), a sudden choking incident (child, tragic), incurable rare cancer of the appendix and so on. A death every few years. Coming to a certain point in life when you realise a funeral could arrive at any moment and it's just better to have a designated outfit, there, hanging at the back of your closet, ready to go. It isn't till a little later that you decide you may as well pick out the outfit you want to be buried in along with a photo of how you want them to make you up. (You've witnessed time and time again corpses made up poorly, lying in the casket looking like they did a decade or so ago due to a poorly chosen photo. Hair, and if it were a woman, make-up that is no longer in style. Best to take care of these things well in advance so as not to shock the viewers and send them into a strange disjuncture of time on top of having to face the cold, hard, fact of death. Besides, it was plain embarrassing to have to go up to the casket and say goodbye to someone like that. Their look so clearly outdated, like someone who walked into a room, showed up for a party with the wrong kind of outfit. Knowing full well that if they were here they'd be nudging you, whispering, *'for God's sake, why didn't you tell me!'*)

At the edge of the asphalt, Lynn waits under the shade of a row of trees picking the skin off the green maple keys trying to figure out which one of the arriving guests is her father.

'Well, *John* is your father,' her mother had said before she left, 'and don't you forget it!' But this was her real father, her own flesh and blood. 'Just don't expect too much or you're going to get hurt,' her mother concluded, wiping the large steel pot she always used for making her garlic mashed potatoes.

On her mother's advice, Lynn had been watching the obituaries. Going up to the corner store each morning, putting down her two quarters to buy the papers she hoped would bring the news. Flipping through the different newspaper sections, turning each light, kind of rough but soft-edged large page till she got to the place where people died and were sometimes remembered. Some of the photos were of people when they were young, even though they'd died when they were old. 'Eighty-seven years of age,' read the words beside a photo of someone in his twenties, a smiling face in a World War II uniform looking proud and alive and full of hope – which was exactly the point, Lynn guessed. A sense of hope for the family, the picture letting them believe that life had been good and happy and worthwhile, rather than having to face the real plight of the elderly – abandoned and alone, not living but just existing, as Lynn's gramma liked to say in her declining years.

Lynn's mom had heard through the grapevine that Joe Logan was sick with colon cancer and probably didn't have long. If Kenny were coming back to town, it would be then. He'd come for his mother's funeral years ago so he'd most likely come for his dad's, if only for his sister's sake. The two of them had remained pretty tight over the years and Louise was the only one who seemed to know about Kenny's wanderings since he'd left Windsor, Ontario, the southernmost city of Canada, and as a border city of Detroit, also the most industrial.

'Ever since he was about fifteen, Kenny was never home. He was always out in a stable somewhere, which was hard to do really. He'd hitch rides out to the county finding odd jobs cleaning barns and things,' Gerald would say, who, unlike his sister Louise, could only reflect on the pre-flight years in Windsor. Like so many of the teenage boys of his generation, Gerald had gone to work in one of the car factories – Ford, GM, Chrysler, it didn't matter which one – quitting school to join up with the night class program at the factory instituted to both recruit young workers, and to help them receive their high school diploma. 'My brother Kenny never could stand *even the idea* of a factory,' Gerald would say, cracking open a bottle of beer to sit out on the back wood deck he and his brother-in-law had built one summer together. Sitting in one of the patio chairs with the all-weather upholstery, Gerald would simultaneously lean back into his chair and his swig while eyeing the case of Labatt's Blue into which he then flicked the cap. The clink of the metal against the glass of the empties always making his wife start, jump a little as she was sent into some remote corner of her childhood on a road not far from here with cheap housing built for returning vets. Like most men on the street, her father alternated between sadness drowned in a bottle and rage channeled through fists that hit whatever and whoever was closest.

'Yep, that was Kenny allright, always off somewhere in a stable.' Gerald would say. One time, at the sister Louise's insistence, they got to see it for themselves. Kenny was living in Oklahoma then and they'd driven all the way there through Michigan, Ohio, Kentucky and Missouri. It was supposed to be a vacation so the kids would get to know a bit of who their uncle was and Gerald's new step-daughter would get to feel like a part of the family. Strangely, it had been Kenny's suggestion. At the Legion Hall, after their mother's funeral, they'd all been sitting around after having eaten their fill of penne with meat sauce followed by broasted chicken and potatoes when he mentioned that they should come down sometime to Oklahoma and see the horses. He had a ranch about an hour outside of Tulsa (it was his wife #1 and her mother's really) and it was because of Gerald mentioning that his step-daughter loved horses that Kenny got started, eventually inviting them all down to visit.

Kenny stretches his long legs out in front of him for a moment before resuming the uncomfortable and awkward crossing and re-crossing of them in the small Legion fold-up chair (unbelievably to the step-daughter, Kenny is even taller than his brother Gerald, standing at a full 6 foot 4). His cowboy hat sits respectfully on the Legion Hall banquet table as the girl stares, curious, at his silver belt buckle with the inset stones – some sort of mixture of black and green-brown specks that matches his boots.

'You'll have to work. Hard. Because if you don't like cleaning stables you'd just better go get yourself a figurine.' Looking down at the ground (he's caught her eyeing the buckle), she doesn't mention that she already has a whole collection.

Kenny takes a drag and places his cigarette in one of the small anonymous white glass ashtrays set out at intervals as those were the days when people smoked freely in all manner of public places and no one thought in the least that they were committing some crime against humanity with each and every puff. 'Yes,' he says, twirling it now a bit to make a little cone shape with the lit burning end, 'when you come down to Oklahoma to visit, that's what you'll do and we'll see how you like horses then.'

'The safest place to be around a horse,' he continues, though it seemed he had been done, finished with what he had to say, 'is right up behind 'em. Right up behind the rear. *Any idea why?*'

The girl lifts her gaze from the square tile of linoleum on the ground upward toward the hat, half-eaten plates of penne and chicken on the table, and then eventually further upward and toward the back wall of the room where the flag hangs downward with banners of poppies and the 'In Flanders Field' poem painted right on the concrete blocks that have been first painted a creamy white.

'No?' he says, 'Well then, come here.'

The girl involuntarily slides her chair near to his.

'Closer.'

She is near now to him, near enough to smell his breath, his body, feel how tall he is and strong.

'If I hit you, *now, I'm gonna hit you* – don't worry, I won't do it hard,' says Kenny, butting out his cigarette before leaning over into her, 'how's that gonna feel?'

The girl sees the ladies who volunteer at the Legion – wives, girlfriends, relatives of men – coming along with the clatter and clank of plates and silverware to clear things away, take everything into the kitchen to wash, out of the corner of her eye.

'Now, get up and go stand over there. And get back a bit. Whad'ya think will happen now? Is it gonna hurt *more*? *Or less?*'

'I don't know,' she said while simultaneously thinking about and feeling the warm sensation he'd made in the muscle of her right arm.

'Well then, let's just see.'

The step-daughter stands waiting, the women still bustling about cleaning, some of them emptying ashtrays now way at the end of the hall, her gaze now returned to the small tile of shiny green linoleum freshly waxed beside Kenny's boot.

'You see that?' he says. 'You got the full force of it. Hurts doesn't it? That's exactly why you gotta stay up close, right beside the thing. Then they don't get a chance to kick ya down, maybe break a bone (if you're lucky), or even get ya right in the head. Now that's the thing you don't want!'

Tears well up in the girl's eyes but she resists the urge to put her hand up to rub the spot where the medium-sized purple bruise is starting to form. Instead she looks down at the sleeve of her forearm, focusing on one or two of the navy stripes of the shirt her mother picked out for her to wear to the funeral. In the end though, it was Pop who ended the lesson by coming over to get Kenny so he could say hi to one of his old friends from when Kenny used to come to the Legion as a kid, accompanying Pop there on a Saturday or sometimes in the evenings after work when the war was still close and real. Pop was a pilot in the war and had wanted to be a commercial pilot when he got home but you had to have perfect hearing which, of course, he didn't by the time the war was over.

They could have saved him maybe if they got it sooner, people said at Pop's own after-funeral dinner/wake at this same Legion (Local 254), but he'd waited too long because he was embarrassed to go to the doctor's. After all,' this same old friend would say, 'you can cut out yards and yards of it before you die.'

Even Louise would agree, their father really could be stubborn. ''Member when we saw him at Smitty's Pancake House that Sunday? He was there refusing to leave even though by that time he couldn't control his bowels anymore and you could smell him from across the entire restaurant.'

'I'll leave when I'm good and ready,' he'd said, finally zooming away on his motorized scooter with the cane tucked in the basket and wife #2 trailing behind him.

'Yep, that was Pop.'

But no one was prepared, least of all the step-daughter, for the actual heat of an Oklahoma summer. Who'd ever heard of 100–105-degree temperatures for days on end? She cleaned the manure out of the stables the best she could and kept close to the horses so that they wouldn't kick her full force and potentially kill her (Kenny's soon-to-be ex-wife had nearly died the year before, getting kicked in the spleen) but it was quite clear quite quickly that when she returned home she would be taking down all the pictures off her bedroom walls, even her very favourite of a mother and foal amid a field of buttercups. The only redeeming thing about that trip, Gerald's wife liked to think, was that her one and only daughter got to be part of a real horse-show like she'd always dreamed.

And though she never said anything to shatter her mother's illusions, the horse-show was really the worst part of the trip. The step-daughter had gone to the show alone with Kenny, his soon-to-be ex-wife, and their two small kids with which she was supposed to be helping out. In the end, Kenny had spent the three days drinking, each evening yelling and stumbling in drunk while his wife #1 scurried her kids around the hotel room, eventually picking the smaller one up and not letting him go while the step-daughter sat there in the corner trying to be invisible and looking down at her new cowboy boots. The last evening, Kenny's rage seemed to increase rather than burn itself out: he stumbled in, punched the walls a few times while slurring and yelling some incomprehensible things mixed with obscenities at his wife before stumbling back out and falling, banging around back down the hall. 'Well, that's that,' wife #1 said, locking the door. 'We won't have to deal with him now till tomorrow.' The little boy in her arms had stopped crying; the older one playing with a toy Palomino on one of the double beds had never really started. He'd remained quite complacent throughout, intermittently looking up and around and then back down to his game as if it all were a regular occurrence (it wasn't till the divorce was final and Kenny was living in Tucson with his wife #2 that the doctors finally discovered the boy was deaf).

*

Her lips had been sewn up or glued together, however the procedure was. That's what you noticed when the make-up was wrong, a decade old. Or in Kenny's mother's case, fifteen fucking years. That bastard did it on purpose is what some people said, while others insisted that grief makes people do funny things, strange things, things that you never in a million years think they would actually do. Joe Logan loved his wife, *dammit*, these others vehemently insisted. And if he got remarried a mere six months after the death of his wife of nearly thirty years, it was because he was devastated, lonely, and it was, in fact, what was best for his health. Even his daughter Louise would eventually agree, standing there in one of the pews unable to think of anything but her mother's Royal Doulton figurines in their pretty dresses with matching parasols or faithful dogs (one given each year for Christmas or some other special occasion like Mother's Day), sitting in what was now wife #2's china cabinet. Even years later after Pop had died, she consoled herself by thinking she could walk over anytime to that woman's house and take back the collection of Royal Doulton figurines that had once been her mother's.

'Of course she'll give them to me, they're mine!' Louise would say, swigging her bottle of beer or sipping the triple Red Ruby (vodka and grapefruit juice in an effort to be healthy) on the deck built by her husband and brother the summer after they'd finished Gerald's. 'She's just keeping them for me.'

The picture used for their mother's funeral had been snapped just after the waitress brought the appetizers to the table. It was Ellen's wedding rehearsal dinner and they held it at Koolini's on Tecumseh Road. Ellen was Louise's favourite cousin and her mother Jocelyn's only god-daughter. Koolini's was new in concept, one of those places with carefully made stucco columns and green plants with mirrors to catch the light and make the place look pleasant and spacious. The desired effect was that upscale Mediterranean look which became so popular in the 1990s, making people feel like they were somewhere else while at the same time validating their choice to stay and live in Windsor. It was at a great location too, right along that stretch of Tecumseh Road equidistant from Chrysler's (the engine plant) and Ford's Foundry with its medium industrial blue smoke stacks that would one day be shut off for good, cranes taking them all apart piece by piece, rusted but still painted blue with people watching from the bar Players across the street until it, too, closed for good (in its heyday, people would say, there'd be a hundred drafts poured on the table all ready for the incoming men just off the day shift, sixty or so if they were coming in for lunch or at break, *it was a beautiful sight to see!* them all lined up and poured like that).

Louise, Gerald and Kenny's mother's sewn-up (or glued together) lips were noticeable in the casket because of the pale salmon lipstick she was wearing at Koolini's sitting next to her god-daughter Ellen and Ellen's then mild-mannered fiancé and soon-to-be-domineering husband Rob. It was an old lipstick, the shade not exactly matching the long, green, leaf-print dress she ended up putting on at the last minute in place of her original long salmon-coloured skirt and white summer blouse. The appetizers – ordered after the usual 4 to 5 minute table-wide discussion of how to correctly pronounce the word 'bruschetta' – ended up being an assortment of wings, dips, fresh vegetables and warm flatbread drizzled in olive oil.

'But who was it that took the photo?' was the question asked by Ellen's mother and her two sisters when they thought about it. Not about the sewn-up lips per se, but about the whole thing in a more general way: their youngest sister Jocelyn's death, the way they didn't get any say in her funeral (not even a single hymn played for instance), and the plain wood coffin just like a pauper. *She didn't deserve that!*

'Well, when you think about it, Joe Logan did kill her, all that whisky in the evenings and never giving her anything nice, not even that vacation to Hawaii she always wanted or painting the bedroom for her, though you notice how he was off on vacation right after the funeral and you saw how fast that bedroom was repainted once he wanted to sell the house!' the eldest sister would say, followed by a long drag on her cigarette. The inhale and long exhale of the smoke somehow containing all the thoughts and emotions just spoken into which the women would float up and disappear until someone (usually the middle of the three) would bring it, everything back down to the sensible and innocuous: 'Well, it was her time. We all have a time, and that was hers.'

Kenny leans in with the weight of his 6-foot-4 frame on the shovel to demonstrate how the step-daughter can muck out the stall more efficiently. That's what he calls it now: mucking out. He takes time to show her how to keep the wheelbarrow near to the door so that she doesn't have to move it there when it's full of manure and risk tipping it over. The girl begins to think he is not unhandsome, and despite the fact that you have to wear long pants and boots in 100–degree weather, she comes to understand the order and rhythm of mucking out stalls, the deep satisfaction that comes from leaving clean bedding, water and food in place of the mess of dank and dirt and waste collected in the dim light of a closed-up space. It's just when the horse is there, watching, that she feels afraid. Listening to the sound of oats being softly but firmly ground between teeth while it stands there, eyeing you, watching the movements of your body walking, bending, arms lifting, waiting patiently for that moment when you'll let your guard down a little and turn your back.

And in fact, it was the Palomino, the one that Kenny had told her wasn't dangerous, just temperamental, that got her in the end; that made her want to forget about horses, even her figurines.

She had not led the horse out because the stall was big. Kenny had said to just lead him to the side while she worked, and to put the wheelbarrow right in the door opening as usual, but also to block him from getting out. She was deep in thought and the rhythm of mucking out when it happened. Somehow simultaneously feeling herself perform the task of cleaning out the stall while being aware of the thing atop of her, its bulk of stomach, ribs, legs lifted for the jump. Its hooves with hard and definite edges the same dark colour as its cock, for the moment drawn up into the small triangle of skin but easily imaginable as emerged, long, semi-hard, hanging heavy like it often did when the horse was standing there seemingly as it always did – chewing its oats and making the same kinds of watchful movements; only now, the cock was hard and long, heavy with its own weight, hanging there ready, out in the open for everyone to see and yet, miraculously, somehow managing to remain unacknowledged by all.

Just before the Palomino jumped over the step-daughter bent down getting ready to refill the trough with fresh, clean water, the hulk of body, hair, skin, deep and masculine seeped in the scent of its own eating, chewing, shitting, and piss, she'd looked up to see Kenny, there, standing at the edge of the fence.

He was watching one of the boarders. The step-daughter had seen the owner before, a young woman. She'd seen her beat the horse while at the same time trying to ride it; coming down hard on it with the crop while holding the reins back tight, the pain writhing around there underneath her, nowhere to go. The horse's eyes rolling around in fear and its hindquarters (despite their muscular strength) unable to absorb all the rage.

Kenny looks up to see the step-daughter looking at him and they find themselves caught, there, together in one of those moments that people sometimes find themselves in – watching some injustice being carried out with the weight of the moment, of expectation that something might be done, spoken: that something might, after all, be changed. Muscles, tendons, an awareness of the power in arms, legs, back neck shoulders, jaw mouth chin, *the momentum of possibility*. Living in that moment – individual and collective – wondering: will anyone (including me) end up taking action? And then (as it often happens) when no one does, the settling into having turned your back on the situation, the unspoken conspiracy, everyone now collectively agreed to the acceptability of the injustice, its normality.

The fence seems open, even though it is there, demarcating a boundary, a limit that cannot be trespassed. And this is because of the wide, open spaces of field that lie there serene and inviting in between rough slats of wood bound together only at certain points by pieces of rigid wire. Kenny watches for a few moments longer before finally flicking his cigarette down and turning back toward the entrance of the stable – the woman's struggle continues on in plain sight.

He has his hat on and his shiny silver belt buckle glints in the sun, but it is his tall lankiness that gives him away to his daughter Lynn, still there waiting at the edge of the parking lot amid the littering, scattering on the ground of maple keys, seeds peeled nervously and torn prematurely from their skins. She tosses a last key down toward her feet, bare in her summer sandals, to begin her walk over toward the mourners.

'Hi,' she says, 'you're Ken, right? Ken Logan?'

Kenny takes a drag from the cigarette he's almost finished smoking the legally prescribed ten feet from the doorway. 'Yes,' he says, 'I'm Ken Logan.'

Lynn sees the lankiness of her own body hidden there inside him, until now unrecognised; the same lankiness and tall awkwardness for which she has felt both hatred and shame.

'My mom said I should watch the obituaries, and that's why I came. She said that's how I could meet you, find you. She's Elizabeth, Beth Dougall, from high school, and she says you're my dad.'

(There are some ensuing dates and years and times and recollections and ums and pauses and looking out toward the lawn of the chapel/funeral home ending with Kenny lighting up another cigarette) while he says, 'yes, could very well be' to which the daughter replies, half-assertive now, 'so it is possible then.'

'Well, it's possible but like I said, even if something like that did happen, your mom would know that I wasn't a part of it.'

Father and daughter look at each other, eyes, shape of jaw, chin, lips, reflecting.

Looking the way someone might examine, see themselves reflected in a mirror. Fingering contours, edges of bone beneath skin with care, observation and finally detachment. The same way Jocelyn, Kenny's (Gerald's and Louise's) mother would sometimes see herself in the mirror when she was alone, or thought no one else was looking. Carefully examining the permanent bump that had formed on the bridge of her nose, the blackened eyetooth which had been chipped in a way that eventually made it go dead (drinking from a bottle is what she told people when someone's elbow knocked it, making it hit hard against the enamel), the small but deep scar above her left eye which (luckily) blended in nicely with the natural shape of her left eyebrow.

'There's nothing I can do,' Kenny says, followed by another drag on his cigarette as he looks out onto Tecumseh Road where the decay of the city is ever more readily apparent (nothing though, compared to Detroit they say, factories and skyscrapers with their storeys reaching high up toward the sky, *abandoned*). Butt flicked down, Kenny puts his fingers, hand and palm over his buckle while the sign from the old Lad's Dairy Bar still stands like a beacon from the 1950s.

The chapel doors open for the last of the mourners. Some, with arms interlocked, still ride the tail end of the sanctioned display of public grief; others, more distant in relation to the deceased, look up at the sky, cautiously commenting on the sunshine, simultaneously wanting to be respectful and to bring people out of it, back to where they have remained: firmly rooted in the everyday. The list of errands to do still there in their minds, trips to the bank, items to be picked up at the grocery store, the detail of construction on Wyandotte Street making them think ahead to the possible alternate routes home.

The asphalt is old and gravelly beneath boots, car tires. Lynn stands there alone at the edge of the lot watching men's jackets being smoothed down, skirts being tucked in. She holds the obituary – softly torn from its newspaper page – while the sun shines, car doors closing on the legs of great-aunts, uncles, cousins, and other people she will never know.

TED & SALLY

SO IT ENDED BADLY. A tragedy.

They went to the grocery store one day in Sudbury and Ted was driving in the oncoming lane so they had a head-on collision. Well, Sally got the worst of it. Ted wasn't so bad but he was in a different hospital than her. Not an asylum, but some place like that. It was then that they diagnosed him with Alzheimer's. All that year before he was acting funny. But it was more his personality than anything else. That was the year Henry and I had them in Florida at the trailer. They stayed with us two whole weeks and we treated them royally. Then, in the spring when we went up to see them in Sudbury, it was like he was mad, being kinda mean and ignoring us. So I said to Wanda, my sister, 'what's wrong with Ted? It's like he's mad. I think that he's being rude after all we did for them in Florida.' Little did we know it was the Alzheimer's. Then he broke out of the hospital they had him in and he walked five miles or more in his bedclothes to where they had Sally in intensive care. But she never recovered from her injuries.

And that's, what done him in.

AND THEN THAT WHOLE
SHEMOZZLE

IT'S HARDER FOR YOU 'cause that's your mom. They say when your mom dies you lose everything. My mother had eight heart attacks before she died. I remember every time she had one we'd all fly in to see her: me, Ted, Wanda, Mike, Joe. When we'd get there, she'd perk right up and get better. She especially loved it when Ted was there. I mean she loved us all but if you told her *Taduez* was coming, well she just loved that! We'd stay a few days, maybe some of us a week if we could. Then no sooner would we step off the plane and get home the phone would ring. It'd be Tommy saying Mother had another heart attack and it looks like she might not make it. So, everybody back on the plane to Winnipeg, and wouldn't you know it, she'd perk right up again. I don't know how many times we done that. Up and down, back and forth. When we were there she was fine, when we left she was about to die.

The last time it was me and Mike who stayed on. Wanda had to get back to work and Ted and Joe left together for

Sudbury. It was the day before we were about to leave and I said to Michael, 'let's go down and have our tea leaves read at the Chocolate Shop.' I used to love to go down there when I was a girl. My cousin Stella and I would go there together. Well, when I finished my tea, I could see in the bottom that it looked just like a coffin with people all kneeling around it. And I showed it to Michael and said, '*uh oh*, I don't like the looks a this, Michael.' As soon as we got home to Windsor, Tom called to tell us the bad news. So we packed up again, but this time it was for the funeral.

And then that whole shemozzle that happened there too. TV cameras, the radio people, all there at Mother's funeral. What a circus! Would you believe it! They wouldn't let her in the cemetery even though that's where she had the plot. Right beside Dad with her stone already there, bought and paid for. Everyone standin' around with the gates locked, them saying that she couldn't come in because she got remarried. Well, what was she supposed to do! An elderly widow woman with no one to look after her, kids moved all away *scattered to the wind like seeds!* And besides, he was a good man, even if his house was haunted. I don't know how Mother stayed there alone for those years after he died. We stayed in it one night and that was enough. It was his son from his first wife who took it back after. I don't know if he knew about the evil thing living there. It was upsetting though, us all outside the gates with Mother in the casket and them saying they wouldn't let her in. What were we supposed to do?

86

But that's the Catholics for ya! It was Joe who called the TV station. Thought that if there was some story about it, they'd have to let us in. And that's exactly what happened. She did have a plot there after all.

How they even thought they could refuse her is beyond me!

THE TWO STELLAS

THERE'S NOT MUCH to think about once she's dead. Just that it's two more weeks till the end of the month and that the cheque should come on the 18th. There's still unpaid bills from last month but it should be OK, they're both on the account. Her Canada Pension is $800 and the Old Age Pension $400. Plus the $300 widow's pension that Henry never thought well enough to sign her up for – Stella and Judith talked about it so much it sometimes seemed they actually had it.

'Even though I looked after him all those years, cooking and taking him to the doctor's every week to have his blood checked, making sure his blood thinners were allright so's he wouldn't have another stroke. If I'd a known I wasn't even on there as his wife, I wouldn't a done it, believe me! He coulda found somebody else to do all that for him,' Stella would always say.

The Visa bill would have to be foregone, its minimum balance far beyond what Judith could ever pay. Months of not making any payments at all, not being able to spare any money until the weight of the phone calls became too great, calls at dinnertime just when the two women were trying to relax, put food in their mouths, the moment when they wanted still, in some small way, to nourish them-selves. Golabki, sauerkraut and kielbasa, *bigos* – or hunter's stew, if it were winter. The apartment faced the Detroit River and even though Stella always did want to live on Riverside Drive, it was too noisy and it was always 8 or 9 degrees below the temperature anywheres inside the city so they always suffered the cold. And the damp. But neither one wanted to move or could afford to. It was enough to complain about it.

Judith had finally started putting $25 a month on the Visa and the line of credit. It would never address the thousands of dollars and more than eighty-five years the statements said it would take to pay it off at the current rate of 21.8% a month and at a minimum payment up near $1,700. 'But I didn't use it to go on a vacation! I used up that amount to pay for my other bills! Heat, water, electricity!' Judith would shout when she was still getting tangled up in conversations with creditors who wanted to make her feel like a bad person, a failure, a loser in life. 'I had kids to think of you know! And now, I've got my grandmother to take care of. What do you want me to do? Shoot her?'

'Oh, you don't have the money?' said the last snide young man in his twenties. Living off his parents' money or still in their basement, Judith thought, though she didn't bother getting into it with him because she knew he too, was yet another casualty. And then there were the others. People in their mid-thirties or early forties incredulous at her situation because it did say 'Dr' on her file. How did they get that information, Judith wondered some time ago – she certainly didn't go announcing herself as 'doctor' everywhere she went. What would be the use? Doctor of Philosophy? Who the hell understands that? It must be because of the student loan, she finally (and correctly) realised. She had to provide proof every year of her enrolment and when she finally graduated and had no more proof to qualify for the 8% interest rate, they must have looked at her status and decided that she must now be a doctor. The client now had a PhD – time to flip that up to the regular interest rate of 21.3%.

Judith remembers Noam Chomsky, the famous linguist and cultural critic, coming one year to the university to talk about student debt and how people were enslaved for the next ten, fifteen or even twenty years of their life, unable to ever be free enough to participate fully in society. The Marxist idea of capitalism wearing down the worker, he'd said, only this was the wearing down of the intellectual, of those people who saw the bigger picture of things, of how things might be changed, how the world might be improved in ways that had nothing to do with money. How PhDs were now living on food stamps and that pretty soon the universities themselves would become creditors, joining the banks in a variety of partnerships. Donations and sponsorships which finally lead to ownership. The University of Toronto, for example, with the Scotiabank Common Computer Banks put in the library during the late 1990s easily imaginable as the beginnings of Scotiabank University of Toronto. Or perhaps Toronto TD University, the more logical pairing since the logo was already so similar – that kind of austere formality hearkening back to pride in British imperialism and all that.

But that was so long ago and so far removed from Judith's present life. At least the theoretical aspect of it anyway – the call for change, resistance, the kernel of Chomsky's lecture. The pragmatics of his prophecy she was indeed living. Sometimes when she and Stella were sitting outside on the balcony of their fourth-floor apartment having their morning or afternoon cigarette and tea, the old woman would sum it up nicely by saying on the exhale of a long, thoughtful drag: 'Well, I'm really disappointed with this whole school thing.'

The only thing Judith could do, really, was to warn her own kids when it came time to go to university. Help them choose programs that could potentially lead to a job and show them how not to get bogged down and caught up in the machinations of the corporate university. The idea of higher learning, enlightenment, of the phrase which still called out from behind the ivy – 'The Truth Shall Set You Free' – carved in stone, a mere marketing tool now with no hope for anything more.

§

The sour cream dough has risen in the old woman's bowl. Judith takes it out to knead before working it into a long coil to lay on the floured surface of a baking sheet. Then she begins to form it into balls. At intervals of six, she flattens them down slightly, flours them again and piles them one on top of the other so that they all fit in the palm of her hand. Folding fingers down and pressing as the dough circles move clockwise round, they are flattened out enough to start to make the sweet pierogi. Sometimes Judith makes them with *powidla sliwkowe* – plum butter jam – inside, but the old woman likes these better. Sugary and sweet, the plum still whole but soft inside the boiled sour cream dough.

Judith puts the dough circles aside and washes and dries the last of the plums. She will make the usual two dozen, slicing each plum lengthwise to remove the pit and then filling each empty cavity with a quarter teaspoonful sugar before returning the two halves together. Each of these will find a home in the centre of one of the small circles, the dough folded over carefully and the ends pinched secure with thumb, forefinger and flour. One dozen for the freezer, one dozen split fresh between them; Judith likes hers fried in a bit of butter, the old woman likes hers boiled. A bit of granulated and white confectioners' sugar sprinkled over all.

Leon. That was the thing that split the two Stellas apart for good. Judith had dug up some of the old photos just the other day when they were reminiscing over coffee after cigarettes smoked standing just inside the screen of the sliding glass door to the balcony. Sitting in front of the old wooden chest where the old woman liked to keep all her pictures. Since Judith had moved in, Stella had spent a number of hours putting batches of them into the extra-large Ziploc freezer bags they got on sale one day at the Price Chopper up on Tecumseh Road near Fontainebleu. At first, she was doing it all secretly, grouping pictures together without telling Judith why. But once she started writing family members' names in her scrawl of blue ballpoint ink, Judith understood that this was part of the unspoken project of the bits of masking tape torn from the roll kept in the kitchen drawer under the dark brown aging microwave beside which her grandmother faithfully kept, for some unknown reason, two flyswatters of orange and bright green plastic. Judith moved the flyswatters to a spot under the sink daily, a spot beside all the cleansers which was, of course, more hygienic, but each day at some unspecified, hidden time, Stella always moved them back. The two women never spoke of this, just as they never spoke of the bits of masking tape stuck to all manner of objects in the small two-bedroom, fourth-floor apartment in Harbour Tower facing the Detroit River. Bits of torn tape with the same blue ballpoint ink and scrawl of family members' names: Wanda (daughter), Bob, Louise and John, Larry, Walter (nephew), Stella (great-granddaughter), Judith, Lucy, Maudie and others. Everything parceled out so there wouldn't be any doubt as to who gets what.

Even if they used the platter with the blue roses, faded now into a teal green after decades and decades of use, Judith would find a new bit of masking tape with the name Wanda (daughter) written on the back if the old one had fallen off in the process of washing, drying and putting it away. In all truthfulness, Judith thought the platter should go to her. And not because of the plain fact that it was she who actually cared about the old woman and took care of her in her old age, but it was because Judith was the only person who knew the stories. The one who bothered to hear them and remember them, fix them in her mind in the same way the old woman had them fixed in hers. '*Partners in crime!*' Judith often said to people in the elevator when she first moved in with her grandmother after her two kids finally left for university and Judith had, in earnest, begun to accept that she'd probably be living the rest of her life on disability. Wanda (daughter), of all people, did not deserve the worn, discoloured, beautiful rose-patterned platter with the two deep chips on the right-hand side. She didn't even bother to know or remember her great-grandmother's name, the original owner of that platter: Madeleine. Madeleine Mokriski. (Judith always felt bad that she didn't know Madeleine's maiden name, but then again, neither did the old woman, or she couldn't remember that far back.)

Leon had come up in a few of the pictures. One at a Legion Hall table with Judith sitting squarely on Stella's lap, smiling for the camera. 'It'd be OK if we cut that part out,' said Stella without mentioning anybody's name or why 'we' should get up to go get the scissors to actually do it. Then, in another, when Judith finally got up the nerve to say, 'who's that man hugging me? He sure looks happy,' and Stella said, 'Oh, that's Leon.'

For years Judith had called that smiling face the mystery man, not wanting to probe around in that period of everyone's life when Stella finally got divorced. Judith had been content to simply think of the mystery man as one of her grandmother's boyfriends before what everybody called at the time her 'new' grandpa: Henry. Henry seemed OK to the eight-year-old Judith – he was tall and dressed well and liked to do things like wash his burgundy car and build whole barbeques out of brick around which people would drink and eat. He seemed OK, but Judith always hated how the new replaced the old and how finally, after the divorce, the real grandpa wound up dead and all, quite abruptly, went underground. The only signs of the past were brief eruptions from Stella, often incomprehensible because of the non-sequential ways in which they were told, or because of the ways they were immediately shoved back down from where they came by still years-angry listeners – her children.

Judith's mother had sometimes held the others at bay and this is how Judith got any details she had, and living with the old woman, struggling along after her own divorce and the bad luck she'd encountered with the whole school business, not finding a job with so much debt after her nervous collapse and months of hospitalization, Stella warmed up a bit to speak things, at least sometimes, in their coherence. That, and the fact that she felt time was running out anyways, so why not.

'That is going to go by my tree,' she'd say, holding a ceramic angel that sat on the cabinet beside the door to the apartment where she and Judith always left the keys. There was a piece of masking tape underneath the base of the angel announcing this as so. 'I already had it planted and paid for the plaque that says 'for my dear children.' They don't let you plant it by the headstone per se, but off to the side down the path. It's not far. The casket's paid for. I already went down there last summer to meet with the girl – I don't remember her name. The old one was Janet, I know that. She's the one that arranged for the tree, where it would get planted. I got the kind you can burn 'cause I'm gonna be cremated too, just like your mother.' And this was the real problem, the real dilemma that faced her now, Judith thought, picturing the old woman there on the bed where she'd gone for her usual afternoon nap. How could she deny the woman the fruits of all she'd worked so hard to plan?

The water boils and Judith adds a bit of vegetable oil to the pot so the pierogi with the plums filled with sugar won't stick to each other. She follows the old woman's ways now without questioning. The little things are there as they've always been – the small ceramic pig that sits atop the edge of the control panel of the old stove, its dials of metal and plastic, the wishbone of a roasted chicken bought ready-made from the grocery store drying in the crook of its little brown and pink perked-up ceramic ear. This has always been so Judith remembers without thinking. The plaque nailed to the wall just above that, a bit grimed up from the steam of food cooking – 'World's Greatest Grandmother,' the ribbon attached to the nail faded. When they boil to the top, floating, that means they're done, the old woman had said thousands of times. Judith puts in only three at a time because the pot is small. The slotted spoon is the one made of plastic, chipped and cracked, that the old woman refuses to throw away. Judith has been meaning to buy a plain metal one from Home Hardware and simply replace the broken one with that, the latest act in their string of unspoken exchanges.

§

The road to the two Stellas went back before Leon or Henry or the first grandpa. Back to the open fields of Morris Place and wooden walkways in front of weather-worn houses (their screen doors with holes), streams and the road that was lined so well with chokecherries, bending down together to collect them in the gathered-up parts of your skirt. The road to the two Stellas went back to Sundays with heavy glass Coke bottles and store-bought ice creams, pictures taken standing amid fields of chest-high poppies, dresses bought to match and a pair of shared shoes between.

The road went back to their mothers' wombs: two sisters putting forth the two Stellas just three months apart. 'We were more than cousins, we were friends!' Stella would say to Judith as they looked out onto the Detroit River, the old woman getting up now to straighten out the plants in the white plastic swan planter at the edge of the balcony after she'd finished her cigarette. 'Would you just look at that!' Stella would continue, her arthritic hands fingering the dark purple petunias with that mild look of disgust Judith knew so well, '*The wind just whips the life right outta them!*'

'We'd go see Jean when we wanted to know something, though. She was already married so she'd tell us the things we wanted to know. A course, you wouldn't dream a asking Mother anything like that! Finally, my cousin Stella went to Dr Stewart down on Rupert Street. He'd do anything you asked. It was pregnancy, a course, that you had to worry about in those days – you didn't dare do anything that would risk you gettin' pregnant! So Stella thought that would be a good idea, going to see Dr Stewart. A course later when she married, Larry was wondering why they weren't having any kids. But she never told him what she done. Why should she anyways!'

Judith had, in fact, been hearing a lot more about cousin Stella since she was dead. Her grandmother would go on about the funeral, who was there, what was said, what everybody ate and wore.

'Stella looked real pretty. She had on a blue dress and inside the casket was that pale pink rose-coloured satin. I wasn't sure if I should go. Even up until I was drivin' there in the car. I thought everyone might see me and think: *Oh well what's she doin' here now?* But they didn't. They were all real nice to me. There was a lunch too after the service, but most everyone's gone now. Even Chuckie. Died last year and I didn't even know about it. I really liked Chuckie!'

And if Stella wasn't going over the details of her cousin Stella's service, she was contemplating the events leading up to it: 'Well, she was in a nursing home but the family didn't want her there. She wasn't doing good there at all. So, it was Chuckie that said maybe Marian could take her since she didn't have any kids. So Marian did take her. And that was good of her to do that, a niece and all. She even took her to Florida one year on vacation. Stella had started with the Alzheimer's then too. When she'd get real bad, Marian said it was like a devil was inside her and she'd have to get real firm with her so she would stop and that devil would get cast out.'

Leon treated the two Stellas equally well. Leon in his dark blue polyester pants, white short-sleeve pressed cotton shirt and his genuinely kind smile. If ever there were a second chance in life, it was to be found in Leon. And this is what each of the Stellas knew because each of them had married and divorced badly, as Judith's grandmother liked to phrase it. 'Marrying Larry was the biggest mistake of Stella's life! One time he beat her up so bad she nearly died. Tossed her when he was done on Auntie's lawn. Marian was telling me too that at the end, just before the Alzheimer's set in, she was living with some guy who didn't treat her well at all. Now, why would she do that at her age?'

Stella had asked it as a favour, the other Stella meeting up with her date Leon.

'Stella, do me a favour. Go down and meet Leon 'cause I have to work an extra shift and I'm worried he'll be sittin'' there all by himself not knowing where I am. I tried callin' but he's already left. Could you do that for me?'

'Of course I can, Stella.'

Leon's mouth down there on her so soft.

No one had ever touched her like that. Not rough and scratchy and greedy and hard. He did it soft, careful and gentle. And it wasn't like he was just somehow slowing things down, some sort of variation for variety's sake. No, no. It was like that's just how he did it no matter what. Soft and careful and gentle. Tender.

'Come here Stella,' Leon said when he was done. Sitting there on the edge of the bed now, feet on the floor, holding his arm out to her, inviting her to climb on top of him. He was sitting facing the large antique dresser with the round mirror. Stella looked at him there, waiting, his words and tone not saying at all, 'Come here because I want to fuck you in front of this mirror,' but rather, inviting her in, telling her 'Please come, fall on me and I'll hold you while we watch ourselves...' And the feeling that he could do that, hold them both safely. The tattoos on the insides of both forearms he'd gotten before leaving for the army, shipped out of St. John's, somehow adding to this feeling of security.

How they'd moved together on the bed next to the night-stand with the small black and silver alarm clock and the lamp with the light green-coloured glass ball just above the switch, he on his back, uncontrolling, giving in to whatever she might do, or want. Then when he'd somehow moved everything so that he was on his knees pushing hard into her as she lay on her back with her calves resting on each of his shoulders and she'd started to cry, he just stopped. Pulled himself out of her, brushing her hair gently back as if to say, 'Hey, it's OK,' looking on quietly as her cries turned into heavy sobs. Who would want to give that up! That was worth having, fighting for even – wasn't it?

'Where are your towels?' Leon had said when they were done.

'In the cupboard in the hall.'

He'd gotten up to go to the old wood door that always stuck and took one out. 'There, we'll get you all cleaned up,' he'd said as he wiped the cum off her stomach and hip. And then: 'I should go. Wait. You want me to stay? You'll feel too alone? OK, I'll stay but I snore so that might keep you up. I don't know if that's what you'll want, to be kept up all night.'

'Of course, I can meet him, and will, Stella,' Stella remembers saying, the smell of sex on her fingers and the aftertouch of Leon's mouth still there between her legs.

§

Judith stares at the pot of boiling water waiting patiently for a few of the pierogi to begin their ascent. The fan with the filter that still needs to be changed whirs along the best it can and, from the corner of her eye, she sees that the light in the corner curio cabinet filled with a Christmas tree somehow made of multicoloured plastic beads and safety pins is still on.

The funeral itself, Judith didn't attend. She didn't have it in her to accompany the old woman and this was something that Stella, for some reason, understood. It was that period when Judith was becoming so obsessed with small things, like change. Pennies to be specific. She had set aside a special zippered compartment in her wallet just for them. Pennies from the good years. The ones she wanted to keep, hold on to. Judith was aware that this would be seen as odd so she never bothered tell anyone but her grandmother about it.

She'd stand at the counter of somewhere, a store, out to buy cigarettes or escape the apartment for a while to go have coffee at the Tim Horton's on the corner of Chandler and Tecumseh Road looking across the street at the field of the Catholic church where she was baptised *Most Precious Blood* while sipping her coffee and reading one of her books. While she liked mostly to reread the books she already had, she had taken to letting a few new things in, mainly fiction. Like that crime writer she'd recently discovered, originally from the Ozarks. The Ozarks with their rocky paths, streams and hidden caves, seems like you could bury anything or anyone out there and get away with it.

In the time it took for Judith to scan her pennies for their dates, she would make offhand small talk with the cashier and pretend that she was searching for the precise amount, like she was taking all that time to do somebody a favour. 'There you go,' she'd say, 'a dollar sixty-five exactly,' giving all the bad years away to the cashier. 'I hope you like pennies!' Sometimes the cashier would engage in the small talk, smiling, taking the change and saying, 'thanks for that, I really was getting low on coin,' but mostly they'd just take it, polite but indifferent. Judith knew too that when things were kind of bustling or busy, the time it took to sort out her change started to annoy those people in line behind her. But ever since she had started to live in the world again after her nervous collapse, this sort of thing didn't bother her. In fact, it was like it didn't even exist: other people and their preoccupations, worries about being late for something or other they deemed important but wasn't.

Occasionally, she came across a few good nickels, but she didn't spend a lot of time going through them like she did the pennies. Only if they really caught her eye. Pretty much anything from the '70s could be considered good and when she got one of these or a few at once, it would be a matter of reflecting on the individual years themselves for particular memories of her life. 1974: the first memory of consciously writing her name beside the date, focusing and concentrating hard with pencil in hand over the ruled notebook her grade one teacher Mrs Copage had given everyone in the class in September. 1977: a good year just because of the way it sounds (that and the fact that double sevens are always lucky). 1975: nice because it was situated right in the middle of an overall solidly good decade, and anything from the early '70s was worthwhile because of the free warm summers of being a kid running around the feel of bare feet on the cement of a sidewalk, grass and then sidewalk again. Chasing, being chased, long hair hanging down loose, soft baby curls growing into straggly little-kid hair knotted in places and falling out of lopsided plastic baby-blue and white butterfly barrettes.

Late '70s, riding your bike alone or with friends. Falling down and scraping your palms and knees. Getting back on. The sting of being alive on your skin. Judith had mixed feelings about the '80s though for the most part she kept holding onto them – the '90s and anything in the 2000s was unloaded onto the cashiers. Sometimes there were special coins that came her way. Pennies from the 1950s. 1953: the year her mother was born. And anything from the 1960s was worth having. Sometimes Judith's little zipped pocket in her wallet bulged too full of the good years in all their varying degrees, and she was obliged to take some of them out, putting them in a small pile on the left-hand side of her antique wood dresser, right next to the picture of the real grandpa the year before he wound up dead.

'Even when Auntie was dyin' – well, she wasn't dying per se, she was in a coma for eight years before she finally died – I'd go up to the hospital to see her, sit with her a bit and if Stella came in, I'd just leave. So, we avoided each other like that. There were the times we'd see each other in the grocery store but we just pretended not to know one another. I didn't have nothin' to say to her and she, well, she'd never bother offering up an apology for what she done. I really liked Leon and she knew that. But it was really all those lies she told about me to him that I couldn't ever forgive. Then when Marian called me up to say: "Aunt Stella, Aunt Stella's been asking for you. She keeps saying, 'Marian, I'd really like

to have a cup a tea with Stella, please call her, will you?'"
But she lost consciousness and I kept delaying. It was on
the Tuesday that I finally bought the red rose to bring over
to her. But I was too late. When I called Marian to say I was
comin', she said: "Auntie, you're too late, Auntie Stella just
passed away not an hour ago." So we missed each other.
Although, she did come to visit me, after; I heard a knock on
the door and when I opened it, no one was there. So, I guess
she came to say goodbye since I didn't go to her.'

Judith lifts the two pierogi out of the pot with the broken
slotted spoon and adds two more while waiting now for the
third one to rise. She puts them in the large, clear wide-
rimmed bowl that has served up countless salads for family
gatherings back in the day when people still gathered. Oil
and vinegar to coat the torn leaves of green, bits of raw
broccoli, chopped tomato, cucumber, radish, red or green
onion, and then small cubes of cheddar cheese. Coated and
salt-and-peppered and set on the table alongside the dress-
ings that everyone likes: Thousand Island, ranch, Italian,
blue cheese, raspberry and poppy seed. When all the pierogi
have been cooked and put in the large clear bowl that can
still hold so many more, Judith shuts off the stove and
empties the small pot of water into the sink. She grabs her
cigarettes and white plastic lighter with the dice on it off
the top of the brown microwave with the flyswatters tucked
along the side to go out on the balcony, alone. She watches
the cars go along Riverside Drive as they always have day
and night. In her lifetime anyway. She looks at the river as

she and the old woman have done so many times together over the years, the two of them together. The sliding glass door to the apartment has been left open. Judith scans the apartment: the corner curio with the light inside that the old woman liked to leave on at night, the cabinet with all the items that nobody wants after she dies – the little Asian girl dressed in pink on her knees with flowers in her hair; the little red and blue Dutch girl with the glued-on head; the Christmas tree made out of safety pins; a set of ceramic containers with an orange and brown mushroom for a top handle sitting on an angle; a fake golden clock with a little crystal heart in it that dangles above the words '*I Love You,*' all things bought at the dollar store or five-and-dime if they were old – the sofa and matching loveseat facing each other over a small table, the base made out of ceramic birds and a clear glass top; Henry's painting above the couch that was really an oil landscape done by his first wife who had died so young from asthma, leaving behind a small child that Henry had no idea what to do with; and the embroidered picture of *The Last Supper* that one of the daughters-in-law had made to try and quit smoking sometime in the '70s under which Judith always puts the new bills. The purple petunias ruffle in the wind behind her as she steps over the threshold of the balcony door.

Judith goes to the closet in the bedroom that was extra before she had to move in. She takes out the flannel sheet with the small dark pink roses on it. It is ripped on one end but, like so many things, the two women continued to hold on to it because it reminded them of better times: Judith of her childhood when her grandmother would take care of her, tuck her into bed on those nights when her mother was in some undefined place and she would have to sleep over. Stella, of when she was a middle-aged woman, young, strong and competent, the start of a new life after her divorce before her. The sheet smells of her grandmother: fresh laundry soap and Downy softener, the musty smell from her knitting and crochet books that have been stuffed in a box in the back of the closet along with her canister of needles, and the soft smell of smoke that has drifted from the spot overlooking the balcony to find its way here. Noam Chomsky smiles out at her from the cover of his seminal 1989 work *Necessary Illusions* that Judith always keeps placed right beside the framed photo of the children on her small bedside table.

As she walks on the cream-coloured plush carpet toward the old woman's open bedroom door, Judith begins to feel it coming on, that unreality feeling she'd had all those years before. The disconnect that left her always tallying up how many steps it might be, say, to the kitchen, bathroom, one of the kids' bedrooms when she was married and contemplating the possibility of her legs, feet actually taking her there. Objects taking on personalities – the pair of her daughter's tap dance shoes that would continuously mock her, their ribbons spread wide in a smile lying across the floor. By the time tap shoes began openly mocking her and she felt like there was a real possibility that she might become a thin sheet of loose-leaf paper that could easily be slipped beneath any door, Judith had been confined to the suburban house outside Toronto where her husband was working. The danger of things like buses and downtown subways removed. Just the one-car garage calling, luring her in from just beyond the kitchen window shutters. She'd not been allowed to go anywhere after she told the doctor how it seemed that there was something stronger than she was, some kind of presence, heavy and inevitable, that eliminated the distance between her and the edge of the platform every time the train approached, flurries of people and coats and things, the smells of their workplaces, apartments, families, lovers, pets, the business of some sort of life that did not seem in any way part of hers all mixed in. 'How could it be my fault if there was this thing there, always pushing me?' Judith had asked the doctor in earnest.

§

So tiny she's become, and thin in death. Not even her at all really, Judith thinks. Just a collection of bones now under thin layers of skin. Skin become thin through the prednisone she took to help her with the arthritis she had since her forties when she became a grandmother for the first time. A corpse is not a person. It's just a remnant, a shell of something Judith thinks that was once her, a woman who used to hug and kiss and love and dance. 'How much you've danced is a good measure of life,' the old woman would sometimes say, smoking her cigarette at the half-opened sliding glass door of their balcony.

In fact, it is so small and tiny that anyone could lift it without much trouble at all. And it wouldn't be a desecration to think of those bones wrapped up in her own flannel sheet, the one she'd slept in winter after winter – her very own sheet-cum-shroud. The bones halfway to their disintegration already after a full eighty-seven years on earth. Hair on her head missing, patches at the top and the back which Judith helped her cover up by combing and arranging the other hair on her head just so before spraying it all with the large can of aerosol hairspray Stella bought on Senior's Day (10% discount on selected items) at the Shopper's Drug Mart up on Wyandotte Street and Pillette Road. Her teeth had been removed long ago when people of her class found it more practical to have everything pulled and replaced with dentures than to keep returning and paying a dentist monies they really didn't have to spare. The veins in her legs collapsed finally after so many years with the stent helping the blood be pushed along up and down around the various paths of its circulation and the half a bottle of nitroglycerin she'd been carrying around since the heart attack she'd had in her mid-fifties still in her purse. Judith looks at the label. The old woman always kept it in the pocket with the bit of broken rosary that was her mother's. A string of black beads from a longer, broken string of prayers. That too kept in there since her mid-fifties when her mother, *Tekla*, had finally died.

Judith wraps Stella up in the flannel sheet with the small pink flowers, a set that was bought sometime in the 1960s – the top sheet with the raggedy edges that Stella refused to throw away. The bottom, its match, sacrificed long ago to a tear that couldn't be repaired. Judith feels the weight of her grandmother lift, flannel sheet warm against skin. Her mind wandering now down to what once was the edge of town, along that craggy path by the water and the once-towering Riverside Brewing Co. with the crumbling red brick and faded paint signs. To those lots, long since abandoned, goldenrod in full bloom.

WALLY'S BAITS

INSIDE WALLY'S BAITS were many secrets. Secret things that went down into the depths of the Detroit River to talk to the fish swimming and somehow lure them out. Back to land, the shore, the fisherman's bucket, net, where they could be safely looked upon and tended to. Perch and pickerel would be poached or fried up with a slice of lemon or a dollop of homemade tartar sauce on your plate, leaving you feeling satisfied and happy, enjoying the fruits of a job well done. The smelt run too, a satisfaction for the sense of abundance and careful preparation. So many smallish bodies cooked up and crispy golden-brown in a heaping pile gathered up in front of you.

'WORMS MINNOWS TACKLE' read the sign on the corner of Mill Street and Sandwich Street before it ran to irreparable decay and had to be taken down by the second batch of new owners. The name Wally's Baits was still kept though, painted in block letters on the bricks above the doorway along with the smaller statement: 'We Believe in Jesus.' Wally's Baits had been there since the late 1950s and people in Windsor and Detroit still remembered Wally personally, so it didn't make sense to change things now. It would be bad for business.

The secrets of Wally's Baits had something to do with the obituary the new owners had hung on the wall beside a photo of Walter when the store had just opened and the sign was brand new, purchased with a loan from Walter's brother Tom in Winnipeg. 'Elsie didn't want me to,' Tom would always relate, 'but what was I supposed to do? I couldn't let him lose that too! Especially after it all being so close after Young Walter. It woulda just been too much to bear. So I put my foot down and told Elsie that was too bad. Her idea of getting a whole new kitchen would just have to wait!' The sign was a beautiful blue, like bright blue water, together with a bright red background and those brand new kinda lights they called neon for the lettering.

Together with the loan from Tommy, Walter had used some of the money people had chipped in for the boy's funeral. Especially the little coffin, child-sized. The funeral was proper, no expense spared but there was some monies left over – people had been generous. That, together with the bit borrowed from Stella (his cousin, not his sister Stella – back when the Owchars and Grabishes were still talking), the sign was purchased and hung, its flashing neon arrow underneath the words WORMS MINNOWS TACKLE pointing the way in.

They'd called him Young Walter to distinguish him from his father. Walter and Young Walter is what they said, not Walter and Walter Jr. as in the Anglophone manner.

Walter and Young Walter: as if a younger version of himself was standing there beside him in the flesh and blood. But since the boy had been laid to rest in the St. Alphonsus Cemetery under the small grey granite stone with the calla lily engraved along with his full name WALTER FRANCIS GRABISH, the dates 1944–1955 and '*In loving memory forever and always,*' the all of Walter's energy went into getting the bait shop up and running.

The building on the corner of Mill Street and Sandwich Street was from the late 1800s and divided into three convenient floors: the level with the window opening up onto the street where some of the first streetcars in Canada had run, remnants of the tracks still to be found there in the asphalt of the road; the basement with its five large concrete vats for the minnows; and the upstairs apartment that could house the remaining members of the immediate family: wife, daughter and infant son.

The apartment above Wally's Baits was bigger than it seemed from the outside. The three windows that faced Sandwich were part of the living room where long tables were set up to count the money or eat when the different branches of the family came together. The side door with the wooden staircase going up, remaining long after Wally himself was gone – dead of a heart attack in his early seventies one night on his brother Michael's couch – also led into the living room, though more toward the back where one of the bedrooms was. The other two smaller bedrooms were on the other side of the apartment in between the bathroom and the kitchen. Walter's days consisted of going between these three levels of existence, and since business had started to boom, he really couldn't complain. 'No word a lie,' his sister Stella would claim, long after he and all the other brothers were gone, 'there would be piles a money lined up with ten, twelve people countin' it all on one a the long tables set up upstairs and a line a customers around the corner still yet waitin' to be served! It's too bad he had to die like that, without so much as a penny of it all in the end.'

Before the bait shop, Walter had a restaurant on Wyandotte at Lauzon. It was the latest in his string of start-up businesses after they deemed him too scrawny to work in the mines in Sudbury along with his two brothers, Ted and Joe. 'Go put some weight on and then we'll take ya,' they said at the mine, but Wally never did. There was the onion farm too in Leamington that eventually failed, part of the series of sit-downs with his brothers at wooden tables with whisky and cigarettes, food ordered in or made by their women while they divined what kind of business would really take off. There were, in fact, big plans for the onion farm – everyone eats onions and there was so much land, the property of Wally's new bride, Myrna. Only there was a falling-out with Myrna's father so Wally was essentially on his own.

Walter always had been the scrawniest, even if he was the eldest of eight. The eight didn't include the ones who'd died. Edward the youngest and the very eldest sister Stella, who died so long ago and so far away that nobody really remembered that she'd even existed. The very first

Stella only materialised in rich but sparse fragments, bits and pieces of worry really that sometimes festered in her namesake's mind. Judith would listen as the old woman went on about the very first Stella, looking out toward the river or sitting at the table watching Judith cook in the kitchen. *'That little girl so smart!'* Judith would hear her grandmother say. 'Do you know what she said to Mother when she was dying? "Don't cry for me. Don't be sad, I'm going to Heaven." My mother named me after her but I sure didn't get any of that little girl's brains!' Judith would listen to this as she patiently and methodically wiped off some of the accumulated grime from the wall behind the stove on top of which the little ceramic pig with the drying wishbone in its perked-up ear from last night's store-bought roasted chicken sat. 'Mother tripped and fell on her and she ruptured her spleen. She fell on me too, both of us right off the top bunk in the boat coming over from Poland but luckily nothing broke then. They were running away from the Russians when it happened.'

The restaurant opened at 7 a.m. but Walter never came in till quarter past 11. The morning rush over and lunchtime just getting set up. Ten tables and ten booths: the place was small but not tiny or cramped, and the windows facing both Wyandotte and Lauzon made it bright inside. Myrna had decorated it with some floral-patterned tablecloths – just for the tables out on the floor – while the booths along the walls remained bare, with their red upholstered seats that had been bought over in Detroit for cheap. It was a good little business, Walter thought, and even people out here in the far east end had to eat (he had preferred somewhere downtown but the rent was too high). He was stretched thin right now but in a few years things would settle down. He'd be all paid up with Myrna's father once and for all, and finally not have to answer to nobody. Not even to Myrna, who'd recently taken to following him to work once the girl and boy were off to school. If she came before 11 a.m., with or without the baby, everyone had their instructions. Even Stella and Ruby covered for him for a time – after all, blood is thicker than water. Besides, she really should be at home cleaning; did you see the state of her house? When they went to visit Mother in Winnipeg last summer, Mother told me that Myrna kept throwing all the baby's dirty diapers into a corner of the bedroom. *Can you believe it! Well, you can be sure Walter gave her hell about that!*

'Myrna, why don't you stay home and clean,' Walter's sisters Stella and Ruby said, 'instead a cartin' the baby around and following your husband to work every single minute of the livelong day!'

Land and the onion farm had seemed like such a good idea. Back when he and his brothers were riding the rails looking for work, owning land was the ideal. Nothing could beat that! Put on weight to go work in the mines? *No thank you!* Leamington was as good a place as any to live, and marrying into land was a good a plan as any, but that was before Myrna turned to fat. And it wasn't so much that she'd turned to fat in a way that definitively prevented

Walter from fantasising about her body as voluptuous, but that it'd all changed and gone in a way he hadn't anticipated. Three kids to support, a father-in-law to pay back a hefty sum of money for all the expenses he'd incurred with the failed onion farm, and a wife who now followed him to work every day besides being there home, at night. Walter had now taken to drinking whisky throughout the day and having a cigar in the evening, in addition to the pack and a half of cigarettes he smoked a day since he was fourteen. He was just in too deep, he often thought, driving across town to arrange for next week's order.

The menu consisted of regular home-cooked meals like meatloaf, mashed potatoes and green beans, bacon lettuce tomato and turkey club sandwiches, eggs and bacon and a pancake breakfast, fried pork chops and potatoes, steak with fries and a salad. Sauerkraut could also be ordered with the pork chops instead of potatoes, and pierogi were popular along with the cabbage rolls Stella and Ruby were paid for a while to make – before Doris was permanently hired. If this business failed, Walter often thought, driving the used 1950 Chevy that he still owed $200 on and blowing the smoke from his Winchester out the rolled-down window, that'll be it. I'll end up like my father, burst ulcers and stomach cancer with not enough pallbearers for the funeral. Doris always told him no, this wouldn't happen, he'd see, it would all be fine in the end.

Doris, her flesh finally let loose in the bedroom of the small apartment she'd rented near the warehouse off

Crawford Avenue in the west end. Breasts falling heavy out of the pointed cups of her salmon-pink size 36C satin Wonder-Bra, the rolls of her stomach freed from the Perma-Lift girdle with the Magic Inset and its new lightweight silver stocking clips. Wally's small but firm hands with permanent callouses from the failed onion farm on the upper part of his palms that Doris always complained about running over the red marks the inside seams of the girdle had made moving down now over her inner thighs that were sweaty from rubbing together under her waitress uniform all day, the dark black hair still pressed flat from her new Pech-Glo panties and the somehow soft but heady scent of her cunt enveloping them both in the two worn-out rooms overlooking the goings-on in the street below.

§

The child-coffin had the crucifix on top with Jesus' arms spread up and high. There were sprays of white roses and hyacinth, and the word *PLAYMATE* was written on one of the ribbons in gold. It was the kind of coffin that was tapered at the feet and, inside, the linen with the hand-embroidered scalloped edges that had been so carefully pressed flat. There was a pale blue forget-me-not on each of the four corners to match the blue silk ribbon in a bowtie around his neck, something which made him look like more of a child than he really was. Doris showed up at the funeral and even though it had been years since the first one she'd been to when she was just the age of Wally's boy, Young

Walter himself, she still felt weak, with nausea rising up when she walked in through the door. The door where death was lying, laid out there in its best for everyone to see. Doris raised by her sisters, no photo of her mother to be found anywhere, like she'd never even existed. Growing up in an era when it was shameful to have your mother die. Like the whole thing was your fault and should be kept a secret; dark, locked away forever, hidden inside. It wasn't until she was well into her sixties that she openly admitted to eating the jam-filled cookie drops her mother used to make her and the three older sisters. 'I think they were called bear-paws,' she'd say, sitting on a friend's sofa, dipping one of somebody's store-bought cookies into tea.

People came to the coffin to see the boy and wonder why. And because it was hard to find any real reasons, relatives, friends and acquaintances commented on the beautiful sprays and how angelic Young Walter looked lying there so still in the casket, one hand holding the wrist of the other, the lit candle on the table and the old black bead rosary spread out in front. Doris went up too to say goodbye though that was the one child of Wally's she'd neither seen nor met. The older girl Rita and the infant son Stan (named after Stanislav, Walter's father) she'd seen in the restaurant that day when Myrna'd come looking. Myrna wearing those too-tight dresses since she'd turned to fat and all her complaining about Wally that had been making him so unhappy. Doris had also attended the funeral in the hopes of soothing Wally, like she had about the health and well-being of the business when he was so worried, trying to keep it alive.

'I'll look after those kids,' Doris had said on more than one occasion, though she truly hoped it would never come to that. Truly she hoped that they'd all stay with Myrna and that she and Wally would eventually have their own. 'Kids really do like me you know,' she'd say in the small but neatly kept apartment overlooking Wyandotte Street and Crawford. But now that Young Walter had died, Wally wouldn't even acknowledge her presence. And it was from Rose that Doris had to learn about the eventual closing up of the restaurant all together. From Rose, Doris thought, of all people! Little backward Rose from Tillsonburg, no less!

Doris remembers all those times when Wally would stay with her, telling Myrna that he had to stay over in Detroit to pick up an order of those things you couldn't get on this side of the river. Wally waking up in a sweat, coming up out of the deep of his childhood in Poland at night. Dreams that came to him when he was feeling the weight and burden of life in a way that no human act or contact could make subside. Dank houses with dirt floors and not enough to eat, the Russian advance on Poland relentless and brutal. The *Konarmia* a kind of kaleidoscope of horses, men with bare feet or shoes made with pieces of old tire and strips of leather holding everything together, winter caps, kerchiefs, ladies hats even whatever could be had, or some with nothing on their heads at all, long hair streaming in the wind. If it weren't for the way they killed, mutilated bodies and left their shit smeared over furniture of the houses they raided, the young Wally would have thought the men were some kind of apparition, ghosts still hungry, unsettled, vengeful and forever haunting them, making sure that they would never be forgotten. And when the Polish forces went to these same houses looking for reinforcements for their own troops, they'd round up the men with their sleeping and waking nightmares of the Bolsheviks. Wally saw and heard men break their own arms on the kitchen table with heavy hammers so as not to have to join the fighting. It was one thing to fight off the Russians in your home and village, still with your family. It was another to be made to go out into the winter to who knows where with companies spread thin and sparse, unsure of anyone's true loyalty. Better the crack and splinter of bones at home than slowly freezing to death in the fields or amputating both feet if you made it back alive. Wally could still see that too, and hear the sounds of the words, syllables of the sledge being summoned for someone's impending loss. Polish, the language of war, of suffering, that no one wanted to pass on to the children of later generations. Warsaw 1920 had left Wally's father's arms useless for the work on the farm later emigration had promised. Stanislav with his misshapen forearms standing at the edge of a field of Swan River, Manitoba that needed to be cleared of trees and rocks, and not ploughed. They'd starve to death was the thought that filled their heads each day and each night, though they dared not speak it. The only hint of their collective fear was expressed in the words of Mother, reassuring everyone that, 'if God can take care of those little birds in winter, he can take care of us too.' They had, after all, lived to see the Miracle at Vistula, the first Stella by then buried hurriedly in the ground beyond the river's edge without any marker. *That little girl so smart!*

The steps to the basement aren't concrete but wood. To the right are the furnace and the coal bin that will eventually be replaced. The concrete vats for the minnows cost $300 to put in but it's the filtration system that's the important and most costly thing. The water with biological filtration already including bacteria so the fish can breathe. But the money Wally got from selling back the tables and chairs and booths he bought cheap in Detroit would take care of that. Myrna cried to see it all go and to keep some of the linens, at least for their own table. The money from Tommy went all to buying the new sign. Rita and the baby Stan, shortened now for Stanislav who'd also died a few years before, shared the back bedroom while Wally and Myrna took the one overlooking the street at Sandwich and Mill. Rita and Young Walter were only two years apart, and that's why Young Walter never listened to her or bothered to pay any mind.

'If you go down to the river Walter, you won't be back in time for dinner.' This is what the twelve-year-old Rita had said to her brother, the one everyone called Young Walter. 'And then,' she'd raised her voice to imitate the threat of their mother Myrna's, 'I'm going to have to tell on you. Tell where you are, tell everyone what happened.' Young Walter stared at his sister Rita from halfway down the sidewalk now, his face one of the several young boys there waiting to do exactly as they pleased. 'We're going to the tracks,' he'd responded, 'not the river.'

'Well, I'm still going to tell,' said Rita, picking up the crying baby Stan from the little makeshift crib placed on the shady part of the wooden front porch.

When Wally wakes up at night now, it's Myrna who's beside him. But he doesn't mind. There's just too much to do. Somebody said Doris was moving back to Tillsonburg. He'd also heard though that Doris had gotten a job at the Lad Dairy Bar doing cash. In any case, whenever she'd phone, he let Myrna take care of it. Sooner or later, Myrna'd put a final end to those calls. The minnows, after all, needed to be tended. Myrna claimed that she'd actually seen Doris walking by the store one day but Wally just took a drag off his Winchester in response before heading downstairs to the concrete vats in the basement to make sure the ammonia levels in the water weren't too high and to skim off any dead minnows. The water is clear and fresh this morning. The new filtration system is working just fine, worth every penny, nickel and dime.

§

Bolsheviks still ride through Wally's nights, though routine somehow subdues his reception. Up and down the three flights, the shouts and cries borne of broken bones, open wounds and children dead in the street become a kind of murmur heard in the creaking of the old bait shop stairs. Soft and muffled now, the fear of starvation they had shared upon arrival in Canada and Mother's desperation at the dry goods store of Swan River: a destination chosen only for the images of beauty, peace and serenity that it conjured up. '*Manka! Manka!*' she'd repeat inside, making eating motions with her hands. No one understood this to mean the flour she was so intent on getting to feed the eight children at home – her pleas were only understood in the small scope of the English word 'monkey' which, when she left the dry goods store in a kind of despair and resignation, the people there made her out to be, scratching and imitating her and the animal like schoolchildren in the play yard.

Even Doris too, somehow seemed to slip away in spite of the last time they had been together.

She was still doing cash and walking by the bait shop till one of her cousins married someone from Minneapolis and said to her, 'Hey Doris why don't you just come down and forget about all that there?' Doris starting to pack up her things in the little apartment above Crawford and Wyandotte that she and Wally had shared, the heady scent and images of their bodies entwined still lingering every time she came home, alone, after her shift at the Lad Dairy Bar. 'Yep, you'd just better get outta there altogether Doris!' her cousin kept calling on the phone to say.

Someone had called that last Wednesday night when Walter had stayed over at Doris' place with the excuse of being in Detroit. They'd called to warn him that Myrna was sitting at the restaurant waiting and that Wally should come back, alone. That Myrna was there to confront them both about the whole affair. She'd even left the baby and

Young Walter alone with the girl Rita so she could see for herself how Doris and Wally had been running around all this time behind her (and her father's!) back. 'He still owes him money you know! This is the thanks me and my family get!' Myrna was shouting, shamelessly shouting all over the restaurant, they said. *'So whatever you do, don't come back here together!'*

And even when the guys Walter hired to catch minnows and nightcrawlers started cheating him, saying they were out working when they were off to have a beer or a nap somewhere outside under a tree – a fact witnessed by Tom himself, come to see how the business for which he'd bought the sign was doing, and, out of a sense of family duty and empathy of the loss of Young Walter, never asked for repayment of what was supposed to be a loan – the only reaction was: 'well, those are good guys. No, I'm not gonna fire 'em. And besides, each one's got a few kids to support.' All became absorbed, somehow, by the sense of routine and the three levels of Wally's Baits.

§

But it was the bruises that finally gave Wally and Myrna away. Bruises that never healed, only migrated from their daughter's different body parts – arms, legs, neck and sometimes to her face. The new young nun from somewhere up north near Pembroke who was called down to take old Sister Magdalene's grade seven class at Immaculate Conception, reporting it. Child Services eventually came to take Rita away and place her in foster care. She was going to have a new family, they told her. Reassuring the uncertain girl of some promised sense of safety and happiness upon arrival. When Child Services questioned some of other family members about the bruises, it was Wally's sister Ruby who spoke up on everyone's behalf. 'We told them time and time again, "don't hit that girl, she didn't do nothin' to deserve that! It was Myrna's fault for leaving Rita alone with all them kids to watch!" And Myrna and Wally would both respond, 'she's no good at doin' what she's supposed to, now is she!' And that would be that. What more could you really say about it?'

Just like Stella, the little girl buried so hurriedly without any marker, the one whose spleen had been shot through and not ruptured by Mother's fall as they'd said time and time again rather than risk the word *pogrom* and all it entailed, the evidence of their collective ordeal was submerged in the secret deep of the past. The only access now the descent into dreams Wally would have of the minnows, swimming two storeys below. Looking into the depths of their little fish eyes that in the dream had seen his lost son, Young Walter, but were unable to speak to him of any possible retrieval. The only evidence remaining, in the end, was the small clipping that the new owners had found downstairs in the basement and then, out of some sense of duty, had hung on the wall. They'd found it tucked in with the original manual for the filtration system of the concrete vats and some yellowed papers in a foreign language which one could no longer recognise or understand. An item appearing for some reason in the *Ottawa Citizen* July 14, 1955 that announced:

CHILD DROWNED. A ten-year-old boy was drowned Wednesday night in the Detroit River. Police said Walter Grabish, who could not swim, went down to the river with a group of seven other boys to play. He pushed a log into the river, and was hanging onto it when he slipped off.

HENRY

HE ALWAYS CAME into the grocery store, you know, as a customer. And he always looked kinda funny – dressed in things that didn't match. One time he was going through somebody else's checkout and we were standing there together, me and my boss, Mr Patterson. He was always saying to me after the divorce, 'Stella, you should go out on a date with somebody, get yourself a nice fella to go out with. Get him to take you out to the show or dinner, *treat you like you deserve!*' And I was always saying I'd had my fill a men. They're all the same. And besides, I got my kids – well, some a them anyways, still at home. But he kept on, saying like that to me and he really was a good person, Mr Patterson, always a gentleman. So finally I said: 'Mr Patterson, see that guy over there? That guy in the plaid pants going through Lillian's checkout right now? Well, I'm gonna marry him!' And wouldn't you know it? *One day I did!* I always thought that was funny.

And then, at the church, that's when they said the name Henry.

'Henry!?' I said. 'What do you mean, Henry! I thought your name was Alec!' Standing there at the altar with everybody looking on. I thought that was deceitful. He always went by Alec but that wasn't his first name, Henry was. And he never even told me! If I'd a known that, there wouldn't have even been a first date. I woulda never even considered going out with a Henry!

That's what Henry's third wife Stella always said about their meeting and marriage that, in the end, lasted over thirty years. The last ten or so were marked by the damage he'd suffered from going in and out of a coma after a series of strokes. It was the loss of vision that affected him the most and eventually led to an existence of sleeping most of the twenty-four hours of the day in the second bedroom of their rented house not far from the old Ford's Test Track. It prevented him from gardening because he couldn't see the ground well enough to do anything. After he'd hurt himself with the shovel twice, his wife banned him from any and all garden tools.

'We can't afford another trip to the hospital!' is what she always said. 'And besides, if you hurt yourself too bad, they might just keep you! And then, off you go to the nursing home.'

Normally he didn't let her scare him like this. In earlier days, he would've just shrugged Stella's threats off while walking out the door to smoke one of his menthol cigarettes on the porch, looking at any life going on in the street while deciding what little odd job he could tackle next. The fence needed painting, the lock on the shed needed some tightening, the patch of garden where the green onions were growing needed weeding. Or, he thought, maybe I just might get out the binoculars for a while and see what the birds are doing in the trees round the backyard. Or drive down to the river and watch the boats.

But since the first and especially the second mini stroke, the threat of the nursing home wasn't just something invented by Stella; it was a fact, something real and true. He could easily end up there – this time for good, and not just for a weekend or so when Stella went away to visit her daughter. 'I'm getting old too you know and besides, I can't leave you here alone. What if you fall?' Henry promised he'd be good, that he wouldn't set foot in the yard, not even on the porch. 'Just leave me something to eat that I can warm up. Or I can even just eat cereal, I don't mind,' he said after she insisted that he could easily forget to turn the stove off and burn the house down with him in it. And he would have been perfectly satisfied too to sit indoors eating from the big box of Raisin Bran, his favourite, eaten every morning for breakfast before his shift at Sealtest where he'd worked for twenty years and fifteen before that when it was still called by its original name of Purity Dairies. But she wouldn't let him, no matter what he promised her – it was off to the nursing home for the duration of Stella's stay at her daughter's place.

Later, when he was in the nursing home for good, he begged pitifully each time he was brought back to the house for a day or an afternoon visit. 'Please,' he'd say, 'I'm not going back. I can't. I won't.' And even though some of his favourite food would have been prepared, with some nice snacks laid out casually here and there – plain chips with the sour cream and green onion dip he liked in the little bowl perched on a clip above the big one with brown and gold autumn leaves so typical of the 1970s when it was bought by Stella's co-worker Lillian for her and Alec's wedding; Planter's salted cocktail peanuts and some mixed nuts still in the shell to crack and scoop out with the nutcracker and matching pick set ceremoniously laid out as one of the items Henry had brought into the third marriage from his second wife Irene – he simply wouldn't touch any of it. And while he could be prompted to take a chip or two from the bowl if one of Stella's granddaughters were there to coax him, the act of biting into each individual chip was tinged with quietly seething rage.

'Alec,' Stella would say when she'd go visit him at the nursing home, bringing a banana or two which she hoped would be cut up into his morning cereal, 'I don't want to leave you here, but what am I supposed to do?' The pronouncement of these words and their sentiment real and genuine. 'I can't take care of you. You're too heavy for me now if you fall. Remember that last time when you slipped in the tub? We were lucky those two guys were out working on the neighbour's roof next door. I had to go and call them both over to ask them if they could come in and help. It was kinda embarrassing but luckily they were two strong guys. What about when it's just me? And don't forget that time you got a bruise and cut yourself falling on the faucet,' she explained while lighting up a menthol cigarette out of the pack she'd brought for him to keep in his drawer. Henry kept his gaze to the ground while slowly smoking it. Stella took the opportunity to continue. 'This place is terrible. I know it is. I don't want to do this,' she said, holding the two bananas carefully chosen for their lack of bruises and bright yellow colour in her lap. 'I know exactly how you feel. If it were me, I'd shoot myself!'

They had had some help for a while from the CCAC, the government homecare program. But it always turned out to be more trouble than it was worth. There was never any consistency with the people who came. One woman who was supposed to help with some housekeeping and chores had scorched three of Stella's favourite blouses ironing and shrunk two pair of Henry's best pants in the wash. Another woman broke a vase belonging to Stella's very own mother, and yet another was too dirty herself to clean anything Stella had told her before sending her back to from where she had come. The last woman, believe it or not, was also assisting a woman from Stella's old neighbourhood when she was young and married to her first husband, and proceeded to both dig up and spread new gossip between the two households. 'If you think I want Linda Mahoney's nose in my business now, fifty years after the fact a being neighbours with her, you're crazy! Just forget it!' Stella said before sending this last one packing.

Finally, the CCAC sent them a young man to help just with the bathing, which seemed like a fine idea. Stella said she had always preferred to do her own house-cleaning anyway so that would be a perfect arrangement. And perfect for Henry too, since he certainly wasn't about to get naked in front of some strange young woman at his age. Tom was pretty good the first few times. It wasn't soon after, however, that he started asking them for spare change for the bus. He'd forgotten his wallet and didn't want to have to walk all the way home. This first fare they gave willingly to Tom – anyone could forget their wallet. But when it went from asking for spare change to asking for $5 with no mention of paying anything back, Stella and Henry saw where this was headed and called the CCAC to complain and insist that they not bother sending Tom or anyone else back there to 'help.'

'If you want something done right, you just gotta do it yourself!' Stella said, repeating one of her old life maxims.

It was when Henry's intentions started getting misinterpreted that the trouble began. His workbench had always been in the basement. His father too, had had one in the basement when Henry was growing up so it was quite natural that Henry would go down there in the middle of the night. That's when he had his best ideas. Barbeques that came to him, designs for the elaborate ones he'd made years before for friends, neighbours, himself, whenever he'd had to move or gotten divorced. Red brick and stone like his father had taught him. It was only natural that he go seek out the trowel. He'd be down there searching around for some things to best implement the vision he'd just had when he would hear Stella yelling at him down the basement stairs. 'Alec! What the hell are you doing! It's 2 a.m.! Get up here and get back to bed!' Which Henry would do, not exactly startled, but feeling like he'd better obey and sort out his tools later. 'I told you,' she'd say, tucking him into the bed in the second bedroom, smoothing down the blue-striped cotton sheet and pale-coral chenille spread, 'you don't get up at night unless you want to get us both into big trouble! What if I go tumbling down the stairs after you? Then we'll both end up locked away for good!' Henry promised he wouldn't get up again tonight or any other night for that matter. 'Allright then,' said Stella, 'now that's what I like to hear!'

If Henry's first wife Josephine had lived, things would have been different, Henry sometimes thought. It was this first wife he had loved the most. When she died at the mere age of twenty-five from an asthma attack, he was truly devastated and at a complete loss with what to do with their three-year-old son Lawrence. He moved in with his parents and took a job as a night watchman on the Ambassador Bridge spanning the Detroit River. It was completed in 1929 and named for the goodwill existing between the two countries it joined. As an ambassador of peace and goodwill, it was the longest suspension bridge in the world until 1931 when the George Washington Bridge in New York was finally completed. Henry worked there for two years. 'Christ it was lonely,' he used to say to those who bothered to listen. 'All alone there nights, and that little baby at home, I couldn't stand it.' He first felt happiness again when he finally got hired at Purity Dairies. They were still using horses then and the stable was located on Howard Avenue at Shepherd. Henry always said the horses knew the routes better than the humans – they knew where they were going, what the stops were, and when it was 3 o'clock, they automatically headed back to the stable whether you were finished or not. It was quittin' time! When Purity Dairies had become Sealtest, some of the equipment and furnishings were sold off and replaced. It was a long old wood table that Henry'd been given for free which he still used as his workbench in the basement.

§

Stella and Henry's best time of day together is still at dinner. Stella cooks one of Henry's favourite dishes and he comes out to eat, carefully feeling his way along the hallway, still in his pyjamas. 'There's no sense getting dressed and undressed if you're just going to sleep all day, and besides I can't help you or lift you like I used to anymore Alec. Just come out at your own pace. But don't forget – washing the sheets once a week is an absolute must! Nothing's going to prevent me from washing out sheets and clothes and putting them out on the line. Pillows too! You'll sleep better that way, everything fresh!' On the menu were mashed potatoes, meatloaf with green beans, baked potato, steak and fresh corn on the cob, a pork chop with salad or sauerkraut, roast beef with mushrooms and gravy, sweet-and-sour ribs baked with some white rice. Henry always said he was a meat and potatoes man. Stella, for her part, loved to cook for him. It was the part of the day that made her feel useful, bringing her back to a time when she had kids at home and a future that was always waiting to be lived. Since he had fallen ill, Henry always ate in the kitchen at the small patio-sized table. The room was cosier and the counters were low, put in for the guy who had rented the house before them who had been living alone in a wheelchair. 'Sit down and have some salad,' Henry would say as Stella served him like he was a customer in a restaurant. 'I will,' she'd reply, 'but don't forget I've been snackin' all along. I like to taste things as I cook!'

Henry's second wife, Irene, had gotten the house and the daughter they had, who, by that time, had started getting hooked on drugs. The '60s did that to people – there wasn't anything particularly special or unusual about it. For some it was a phase. For others like Henry and Irene's daughter, Jodie, it was more lasting and even permanent. They all began to lose track of each other after the divorce and then completely after Jodie had gotten pregnant, cleaned up, pregnant again and started bringing both kids to the bar until Social Services found out. Then both were taken away, 'for their own good,' said those at the bar who knew who had called Social Services on her, but wouldn't say. People sometimes still reminisced about it over a drink on one of the last old long wood counters in one of the last old hotels in the city – long after people stopped even using the word hotel to describe a bar such as the one on the corner of Wyandotte Street and Parent. The Wyandotte House it had once been called; also The Happy Tap. And yes, it had always been seedy, people said sipping their beer to those who might have cared to ask. The kids were probably the product of that period of when she had to resort to prostitution, these same people said if they were on the old topic of Jodie and her kids. When Stella wanted to really take a dig at Henry, she brought all this up without leaving out any of the minor but nevertheless savory details.

In fact, that day when Henry was going through Lillian's checkout at the grocery store, his divorce from Irene had become final. He was starting to feel comfortable again in his new routine of being a bachelor. His first son was grown by then and had gone off to Australia to live after having met a woman there when he was on vacation. Henry's parents had long since died and left him a small sum of money from the sale of their house that he had split with his brother still living in Tillsonburg. Irene had gotten the house and most of the furnishings, but Henry was content now with an apartment – his responsibilities ended when he paid the rent he thought, and he had only another five years or so till retirement. Time to enjoy life, maybe go on a cruise like he'd always wanted to Mexico. If he asked Lillian out, it would just be for some fun. No more buying houses, that's for sure!

'Stella, I'm gonna do you a big favour!' Lillian had said. 'Next time that guy in the plaid pants comes in, I'm going to tell him you might be interested in going out to the Legion with him on Saturday night for dinner. He asked me, but

I told him I'm already going with someone steady.' And once Lillian had also told their boss Mr Paterson the news, Stella could not really refuse this date.

'I'm certainly not looking to get married again!' said Stella.

'Well, who said you got to get married? Just go out and have yourself some fun!' Lillian replied. It wasn't long though before old-fashioned rules and a sense of propriety kicked in and even Stella's own kids eventually told her: 'Well, so what do you mean? You're just going to keep on dating new guys?'

§

The misinterpretation of Henry's intentions, the loss of vision that prevented him from gardening, watching birds or seagoing ships passing by on the Detroit River, or from later venturing off the steps of the front porch to look around a bit while smoking his cigarette, made this time of day all the more tenuous. Stella and Henry's dinner hour was enjoyable for its sense of normalcy, but it also seemed somehow dangerously thin and stretched through the day's sense of interminable time. For instance, they had already carted his old console TV away – another of the few things he'd taken from the house with his second wife Irene.

'It doesn't work anymore! The tubes are shot and you can't buy or replace them because they simply don't make them!' Stella's kids had insisted. He had made it out to the curb with the intention of somehow bringing it back in, but it was too heavy. And when he'd tried to start the car one day so he could help out with clearing the light snow falling on the driveway, he'd not put it in gear properly and ended up getting knocked down by the open driver's door and suffered a slight concussion. These were just some of the things that kept him now all day in his pyjamas.

'The guy in the bed next to you is only sixty,' Stella would sometimes say to try and cheer Henry up. 'Think of that! Poor guy only sixty and in the same place as you. He's not going to be going anywhere neither – no family, not able to take care of himself. Look how he's hooked up to everything too when you're feeling sorry for yourself. You didn't have to have that and you still don't now,' she'd say as they smoked their two cigarettes out in the little nursing home garden patio. 'Have they been giving you the bananas in your cereal like I asked? You know, I noticed one of your shirts is missing. I swear they steal things in here! I'm going to see about bringing you home for Saturday. And I've really got to figure out something for the lawn. There's no way I'm going to be able to rake all the leaves from that big tree this year all alone. I wish the landlord would just cut it down. I can't be asking my kids all the time for things – they got their lives to live too. I don't know what I'm gonna do. I want to stay in the house as long as I can but they're already talking about putting me in an apartment.' Henry takes a careful last drag, drops the butt and then crushes it underfoot with a slow side-to-side motion without saying a word. 'I'm really gettin' scared about it all to tell you the truth!'

Stella and Henry sit together, both still now, jointly watching a visitor pushing one of the residents in a wheelchair back inside. Henry's walker is beside them with his name written in bold letters on a piece of masking tape stuck to the cushioned seat.

'What am I going to do?'

When Henry's first wife had died, the first thing he had to do was purchase a plot and gravestone for his young bride. They showed him some options at Heavenly Rest and in the end, he'd bought three plots instead of just one. One for Josephine, one for himself and one for their young son, Lawrence. He wanted to be prepared as a family, he had said to everyone, to know exactly how they'd all end up – together. But Larry said he wasn't going to be needing that plot since he'd moved to Australia. He doubted he'd ever even set foot back in the city where he was born. So that left one plot free because Henry was always reluctant to sell it. Even before Henry started falling and searching out the tools in the basement with which he once put his ideas into motion, he and Stella had decided in a moment of pragmatism that she would take the plot, and that Henry would be buried between his first wife and his last. Plots were well over $10,000 these days plus the headstones and any kind of engraving you might want done. Plus the service and the lunch you could have done now right there, all in the same facility. Of course, Stella complained: 'What! King Farouk between two wives and me one a them! Now who woulda thought!' But in the end, she came to accept this plot and went about making the arrangements for her and Henry. A small piece of earth among others, passed by on a daily basis by travelers on the new highway put up on what once was the outskirts of the city and a leisurely country road never thinking it even possible as they drove along in their SUVS toward endless suburban sprawl, that they too would one day grow old and have to die.

THE NEXT SHIFT

THEY TOLD HER she'd have to sign or she'd be fired. And after she signed, they made it clear that if she told anyone about what had been said and done in that office, she'd also be fired – on the spot.

'But what'd ya expect, Ma? You know they have no union.'

Lillian told her daughter that she didn't want to discuss it and that if Lorraine let any of the other family members know, Lillian would disown her.

'Ten years of service and this is what I get! Hauled in like some snot-nosed kid without even an ounce of respect! I'm seventy years old – that alone should count for something! Don't you think I know something about running cash, running a store! Hell, I was making up schedules for all the cashiers at Dominion Store before he was even born! Asshole. Talk to me like that will he? He's lucky I didn't shove my foot up his ass!'

'I know Ma. It's true what you say. But it's also true that you have a bit of a mouth on you. I told you before. You can't go around saying what you think to everybody all a the time. Sooner or later it's gonna come back on ya.'

'Well, someone tattle-taled. Probably Jenny, that little witch from lingerie. She's always got her nose in everyone else's business. She was the first one to ask me what happened when I came out of Don's office. I just looked her straight in the eye and said, "Jenny, that's really none of your concern."'

'What'd she say?'

'Nothing. Just went back to rackin' brazeers.'

Lillian takes a long drag off her cigarette. It was her third since Lorraine had come over from across the alley for tea. Du Maurier regular fliptop: the red package sitting squarely on top of the little white wrought-iron patio table with two chairs used as a breakfast table in the kitchen. There had never been a time when her mother hadn't smoked, hadn't had a cigarette in hand. There was a story of how she once tried to quit – must have been thirty-five or forty years ago now.

'Lorraine, you should remember, you were about ten when Pepper died. She was so smart that little dog, just like a person! I'd be getting ready for work, up at 5 a.m. to start at 7 a.m. I'd have all the kids' lunches ready, everything set to go. I'd have my bath first, put on my face, get dressed in my uniform and then do my hair. And she'd watch me, and keep me company, and never bark. She wasn't stupid that dog you know and never, not once, made a mess. She'd just sit there by the door if she had to go and wait for me to let her out. Anyway, it was a day when Lucy gave me a ride home, 'member that 1965 Buick she had? Well when we pulled up, there was Pepper on the road – *dead*. Judy Mahoney came out from next door with her apron on and saw me crying. She told Lucy to go on home, she'd look after me, take me into her place for a bit until I was feeling better. The kids wouldn't be home for an hour. Judy made us a nice tea and after I'd finished crying, handed me a cigarette while lighting up hers and that was that. I never tried to quit again. I felt like the two things were linked somehow, my quittin' and the dog dyin'. Like I was being punished for something.'

Lorraine touches Lillian's hand resting on top of the table. Soft purple veins pulse with her mother's blood just below the surface of the skin. 'You should stop work anyway Ma, you're seventy now.' Lillian looks out the back window at her garden. A row of red hibiscus lines the four-foot chain-link fence that the landlord put up last year. They look through the smoke Lillian slowly exhales through her nose and mouth, out past the pastel butterfly curtains she bought with her employee discount.

'I should feed the birds,' Lillian says, 'see how they wait? They're used to me feeding 'em.' She gets up, leaving the cigarette in the small, glass ashtray to burn and reaches into the fridge for two slices of bread. She picks off a corner and puts it into her mouth. 'I'll be depressed if I quit,' she says, chewing. 'Feel like I'm no good anymore, useless. What am I supposed to do? Stay home and knit?'

'Well, that wouldn't be such a bad idea. You've worked hard Ma. All your life. Raised five kids on your own, always had a full-time job. You've paid your dues. What do you want to be a greeter for now, handing out buggies to people at Walmart? Before you know it, it'll be winter again and you remember how cold you were last year at the door, how sick you got after working all those extra hours at Christmas? I know Veronica would really like an afghan and I'm sure all the grankids would just be happy with a hat and scarf, a handmade hat and scarf from their Gramma.'

'Oh, for crying out loud! I'll make the damn afghan and hats and the scarves! I've already knitted three baby caps and sweaters for Linda in case she gets pregnant and I'm not around to see it! Don't you know it's people I need! I need to be out, I need to feel alive, OK? Even with some-one like Jenny, you know? She's nosy and she can be a little witch but we've had some nice chats over coffee just before our shift. And Melissa too, from stationery. She's a nice girl. She's always got time to have a cigarette with me and tell me some of her news. Don't you see Lorraine, I need to talk!'

Lorraine doesn't say anything, just sighs, fingering the package of Du Maurier fliptop on the table. The birds sit on the wires, waiting. Lillian slips on her navy blue Isotoners with the faded satin bows to go out on the small back cement porch covered in dark grey indoor-outdoor carpet-ing. The old metal screen door slams behind her.

From the window, Lorraine watches the birds. Blue-black starlings and brown-headed cowbirds flock to the lawn at her mother's feet. She knows that action of her arm, tossing, spreading things out, tearing things into little bits so everyone will have enough to eat. She knows that gesture of her mother's, her tiny 5-foot-2 105-pound body that will not give in to anything, not to some fifty-odd years of smoking, to the birth and raising on her own of five kids, to the double shifts of bagging people's groceries and housework, to the insults and blows of her gambling husband who sometimes remembered to come home while drinking himself to death, or now, to the harassment of some guy named Don down at Walmart.

'What can I say? They want to get rid of me. I'm old,' says Lillian stepping back into the kitchen and rubbing her hands lightly together to get rid of any crumbs.

'Ah Ma, I don't know. That's why I say, maybe it's just easier if you quit yourself, before that happens. You don't need the aggravation of them putting you through this, do ya?' Lillian sits down, butting out the cigarette she left, almost now all ash.

'Well, I will tell you one thing. That idiot Don's got another thing comin' if he thinks he's gonna scare me. Talk to me like that, *Mr Big Boss*! That jerk doesn't even know how to make up a schedule and I've told him so to his face at least a dozen times. "Don," I say, "don't you know how to rotate people? You gotta make it so that everyone gets the same number of hours and equal, good shifts. When I was Head Cashier at Dominion Store, I had my schedule made up like that months in advance." And that's why he doesn't like me, 'cause I know how to do the job and he doesn't.'

'Regardless Ma, he's the boss.'

'Yeah, I guess. The asshole that he is.'

*

Lorraine remembers Pepper only vaguely. A little brown and white dog playing, running out in the yard by her mother's rose bushes. Red and yellow climbers sprawled over a peeling white wooden fence. Lillian had started them growing from a clipping under a glass jar. Clippings that had grown large into bunches of flowers and leaves embracing, holding the little three-bedroom house on Larkin Road by the old Ford's Test Track together. Lorraine remembers Pepper at her mother's feet, following her along as she walked around the yard on Sunday mornings in the summer, a cup of tea or unlit cigarette in one hand while the other caressed blooms, searching for dead flowers to snap off deftly between thumb and forefinger. Her mother would come into the kitchen renewed, saying how much her garden loved her, how well her beautiful roses grew, their slender yet gnarled roots rising up delicately from the ground. How everything was good and she felt just fine, wouldn't they like their breakfast now before Mrs Mahoney came over for coffee with her two girls to play? She would set out cereal, milk, orange juice and make toast while humming along with her Polish polka music coming from the small radio on the shelf above the stove. There was nothing really to worry about after all.

Lillian reaches for her red fliptop box of Du Maurier and lights up another cigarette. She watches Lorraine put on her shoes by the back door, getting ready to go out back across the alley.

'I'll call ya later Ma, see how you're doing, OK?'

'Yeah sure, thanks hon.' The smoke rises, moving in and around Lillian's face and hands, held there softly in her mouth, nose, chest, soothing. She gets up to find her knitting needles, checking the calendar pinned on the wall by the stove – looking for her next shift.

GO ASK ALICE

WHEN ALICE STARTED making more money writing essays for students than the universities paid her for teaching courses, Alice knew there would be no turning back. Even though ultimately she still believed in the dream of @U (fill in the blank with your institution of choice) and the promise of @YOU (student as consumer and client), there would be no going back because more money was needed, plain and simple. The money Alice made legitimately within the academy couldn't cover a rat's ass. Hell, it couldn't even pay living expenses for one in a furnished room. Support a family? No way. If Alice hadn't finally managed to procure child support, she and the children would have ended up living in a shelter. And for what? A measly worthless *PhD*?

Alice remembers when she won her grievance – one of several she had filed against the very institution that had granted her that useless piece of shit-ass paper they called the highest of all academic degrees. Up there somewhere in that office tower or hotel board meeting room the Institution rented out to wrestle with union grievances. Two separate rooms actually, with a highly paid smug-looking independently contracted mediator. This particular mediator was supposed to be one of the very best in her field at that time, or so Alice was told. Going back and forth, back and forth between the two rooms, straightening out her shirt and expensive pair of red suit pants.

Alice had made them admit, write down her qualifications as part of the settlement. She had applied to teach a course in Women's Studies, for which the qualifications had cost her extra years of her life, study, research, time away from her own kids, and had contributed directly to the eventual breakup of her eleven-year marriage. And instead of hiring her for a course she was absolutely qualified to teach (*'Christ, they were the ones who issued the damn degree!'* she'd shouted at the mediator who was busy making her way now into the other room), they hired someone with no qualifications in the field with the excuse of 'interdisciplinarity.'

'Well, Women's Studies *is* interdisciplinary, isn't it?' one of the Institution's two female provosts said to her smugly but without looking at Alice directly from across the other side of a large antique desk (the Institution had ten of these senior administrators in total whose collective earnings shot well into the several millions of dollars). 'People from other fields can cross over quite easily into it, no?' she'd continued on, getting up now to walk around behind her desk, stopping at a shelf with something on it, looking with interest at some institutional plaque. And then, adding insult to injury, the union rep started chatting the female provost up as she, herself, was now on her way to some other position much closer to the bosom of the Institution.

'Hey, hey! I'm not quite done here, Charmaine!' Alice had said. 'Do you mind?' 'Oh, oh,' Charmaine had said realizing her error. 'Yes, I should have asked you that before I went on to other matters. Yes, you're right.' (Alice later learned from someone outside the union that the woman who was hired to teach the course was indeed a relative of someone in administration – Alice never stood a chance.)

Both the mediator and the female provost, and the union rep for that matter, reminded Alice of the female lawyers she had had before she finally went to Mr Katzman, the only one who had actually given a crap about helping her. They were all just as insidious as the judge, also a woman. All trying to prove how tough and manly they were by being extra hard on the women who came before them. 'All a bunch of stupid fucking cunts,' Alice had resorted to saying more than once. No spousal support, minimal child support (Mr Katzman helped her get an increase when it was revealed that her husband had lied about his earnings and income), and again, adding insult to injury, the judge had forced Alice to enter into an agreement with her soon-to-be ex-husband to 'check in' regularly with him regarding the completion of the damnable PhD! This was just too much to bear. Alice insisted through Mr Katzman that the judge listen to her speak privately, without the other party present. And even though Alice explained that every application he had ever submitted – from citizenship to undergrad to graduate school and beyond – was written by *yours truly!* and that the time taken off to child-rear and even home-school was again done by *yours truly!* that bitch ultimately did not flinch or move an inch. Sure, Alice saw a sign of that female sinking feeling, 'oh, yes, I've been there too,' but ultimately the building and the desk in front of her gave her too much power for that feeling to last very long. Instead, down came the gavel! *Judged and sentenced.* Years later Alice's grown son would say to her quite earnestly, his tone both honest and sympathetic, 'but Mom, what has feminism really ever gotten you?' Alice found that she couldn't defend herself or disagree because he was right. It hadn't gotten her shit.

Sometimes the essays she wrote were for former colleagues, most of whom were on contract themselves. Students forwarded on their syllabi and instructions and Alice would read all her former colleagues' cute little sayings and attempts at getting students to like them or think they're fun or funny or great teachers or should be relegated to the 'hot' category on ratemyprofessors.com. Pathetic. Such sad pathetic attempts they seemed, writing now from the other side. Universities looked like pimps and contract faculty their whores.

One of the real breaking points for Alice involved social media. She was working one of her three independent contracts that year in the Writing Centre of the Institution. A young woman had come in for the 45 min session she had booked online. Alice remembers what she told a friend of hers when she first started working there. It's a kind of therapy really, students are simply stressed out about all their worries – specifically the 25 grand worth of debt in student loans which was the national average for a four-year program when Alice was working that particular four-month contract. Students were visibly unhinged over this, sometimes to the point of paralysis or shaking at the thought of failing or doing poorly while having to borrow all these funds simply to go to school. The Institution had responded by bringing in dogs and cats for them to pet during exam periods, mid-terms and finals. They also set up giant bouncy-castles outside when the weather was nice with some of their corporate sponsors handing out samples of food. But the results were limited. Alice even had a few students passing out from anxiety in her sessions. It was impossible to keep up with all the notifications and special accommodation letters coming in from the newly expanded student services and student accessibilities office: needs more time for assignments, suffers from anxiety disorder, depression, and all manner of other conditions documented by medical doctors. 'And what about my conditions?' Alice often thought. 'Who cares about them?' No one of course, was the answer. You're not a paying customer.

When the young girl had come in for her session, Alice prepared the multi-use anonymous office as she usually did to look welcoming and inviting: opening the half-broken blind so that the view of the trees in leaf would be exposed. It was spring, she remembers, just the light green beginnings of leaves were present, all feathery with some of those yellow bushes that actually flowered getting ready to bloom off in the distance. The desk was cleared with the paper stacked neatly in piles, a dictionary ceremoniously laid out to create a certain kind of mood rather than for actual use, and toward the far end of the desk by the door so that they could be handed out with one of those small pencils used to keep score in golf or mini-golf, the evaluation sheets of Alice's 45-min performance within one of the five of the Institution's Writing Centers. Did the client/student feel satisfied or not? Alice sat back in her chair in a way that was professional and yet relaxed so as to help defuse any tension, her 'teaching clothes' on, – one of two outfits she'd bought to alternate with pieces that could mix and match (the rest of the time she wore what she could really afford, second-hand clothes from the Bibles for Missions Thrift Shoppe) – and waited for the girl's story to begin.

Was it issues getting started with research? Trying to work on an effective introduction and conclusion of an essay? Revising sentence structure, flow and unity of a literature review? Or simply getting your notes organised to begin the initial stages of the process of writing? None of the above. Instead, the girl held out a piece of paper for Alice to read and said, 'Can you help me with my tweets?' At first, Alice didn't understand. In fact, since this was long before Alice knew about tweets and most certainly part of what she now called her pre-Twitter days, Alice literally had no idea what the girl was talking about. She took the paper, but still didn't understand. There were only three sentences on the whole sheet. Alice didn't want to alarm the girl or make her feel embarrassed as she was a foreign student (Alice had once been a foreign student too in another country a long time ago and she knew how it was to struggle away in another place in a language that wasn't yours). 'Do you have the assignment sheet with you? Let's have a look at the instructions.' She waited for the girl to bring them up on her computer screen so they could look at them together on her lap. But this, still, did not make any sense. The instructions were from the Faculty of Science and seemed to be asking students to create three tweets about three different three-year studies that had recently been carried out.

'My professor said not to forget to make them interesting.'

'The tweets?'

'Yes.'

'And the tweets can only be a hundred and forty characters not words each?'

'Yes.'

'And each tweet is supposed to talk about the scope and findings of a three-year scientific study?'

'Yes.'

Looking at the girl as she spoke, her face so open and earnest, the sheet of paper with the lone sentences called tweets still there in her hand, and the girl's laptop open there waiting with the instructions from someone in the Faculty of Science, Alice began to understand. She had been put on. The whole fucking thing was a joke and the whole time she, and now this young girl and other young people like her, had been and continued to be ripped off.

That's not to say she hadn't had doubts; glimpses of what was really going on before. Alice had seen time and time again how students who didn't speak English well enough to follow university-level lectures were both recruited and enrolled for their tuition money – which was more than double the amount for someone classified as domestic. This had been particularly acute within the Institution's School for Business and Management where she once worked on a year-long contract for three years teaching writing for business students. An alliance had been created by someone in the Writing and Rhetoric program so that their program wouldn't go under during the annual budget slashing in the humanities. 'We've got to show we're relevant to business,' the head of the Writing and Rhetoric program coached everyone, 'or we're done. *Kaput.*' A script with an hour and a half running time was drawn up and distributed among the contract instructors. Handed the script that she was to read to the class, Alice diligently went through each of the PowerPoint slides with the three hundred and fifty business students who simply took a picture of each slide while they continued to chat among themselves.

Sometimes, Alice would forget herself and deviate from the standardized lecture she had been hired to deliver. Sometimes, she started ad-libbing about things like the psychology of advertising, the dismantling of the welfare state, the rise of corporations and the active elimination of the public sphere. One time, she went so far as to say that the term 'corporate citizen' was an outright lie, an impossibility, as the definition and etymology of each of the two words were antithetical, complete opposites. 'And here, we've got them actually being used together, in one term!'

she remembers railing on, hands raised, the young people looking at her curiously. Those who could speak English well enough to get into such discussions also did not understand Alice or her excitement. 'If you need it, just get a corporation to give you money, what's the difference?' one young man had finally declared with the other young people nodding and agreeing with him as he sat back in the expensive auditorium chair that was, indeed, furnished thanks to one of the Institution's own corporate investors. Alice remembers how she stood there alone with the PowerPoint and the letter she was supposed to be rhetorically analysing from the CEO of some company at the end of the first quarter, coming to the realisation that she'd better stop deviating from the pre-prepared standardized lecture she and the other instructors were delivering if she wanted to finish out the term. After all, she and her kids needed the money – grade eight graduation for her daughter was just around the corner.

Ultimately, students simply did not have the time, stamina or language skills to write their own university papers and this is why they were being contracted out to people who either were, or used to be, on contract within the universities themselves. But most people don't know anything about this phenomenon. They assume their nurses, doctors, city planners, architects, social workers and any manner of government employees or politicians are doing their own work, earning their own degrees. Just as they assume that everyone working in an institution of higher learning is working in education rather than in stoking the fires of the capitalist machine. Alice, however, knew that nursing students were currently the biggest client demographic of the essay-writing business and that by now, in the second half of the second decade of 21st-century teaching, it was a well-known fact that over half of university or college courses in the country, as well as in the US, were taught by PhDs on contract with no job security, pension or benefits in sight. The best that someone could hope for in the new gig economy was what they were calling a 'permanent contract.' Alice had even seen people getting all excited at the prospect of being exploited on a more permanent basis. People at union meetings discussing who would be next on the list to submit their names to the administration – positions that literally paid less than one half of what the old, regular permanent professorships had. And in the summer months, they would all go on employment insurance or EI as it had recently been rebranded from the negative-sounding but far more accurate because it actually said what it really was... *un*employment insurance. In fact, Alice's friend, the one who was hooked on fentanyl long before it became fashionable or even a national crisis, had gotten one of these newly coveted 'permanent contract' positions in Women's Studies.

'Well, it's pretty good. At least I don't have to re-apply for each course every three months. And, there are some partial benefits they offer after you've been there for eight years. I'm gonna need that for my anti-depressants. Especially since the generic ones for me cause so many different kinds of side effects.' Louise said, telling Alice the good news.

Louise and Alice had started graduate school together way back, moving up to what had become condo city where the cheapest rents now meant people couldn't eat. And even though they went to two different institutions, supposedly the best in the entire country, those were heady days of shared enthusiasm and long talks late into the night. Alice still had Louise's copy of Joanna Russ' not-so-ironically titled *How to Suppress Women's Writing* on the shelf of her bookcase along with Julia Kristeva's *Revolution in Poetic Language*, *Black Sun* and *Strangers to Ourselves*. All were bought at the now-defunct women's bookstore that had been torn down to make way for a seventy-eight-storey combination school/ condo. The school occupied the first four floors and was the compromised result of the lawsuit some parents had filed against the developers because the condo – originally across the street from Edward Street Elementary – would permanently block the children from ever seeing sunlight again. Three random volumes from the seven-volumed *The Diary of Anaïs Nin* were also bought there and stood beside Louise's copy of Joanna Russ. It had been two years now since Louise had accidentally OD'd on a used fentanyl patch they'd found all soggy and chewed on in her mouth when she'd collapsed on the hallway carpet presumably in the middle of the night when she'd gotten up to either go to the bathroom or to get a glass of water. Her girlfriend, passed out from the bottle of wine she drank herself to sleep with each night didn't find her until 11:30 a.m. the next day.

Louise had all manner of methods for taking her various mixes which went way back to adolescence. When Alice's eleven-year marriage fell apart, Louise took the bus over to help her move into an apartment closer to the institution when they were still graduate students. But instead of unpacking boxes or putting things on shelves, in closets, toilet paper under the sink, Louise took out all her paraphernalia to smoke hash oil and pot on the couch, considering the various ins and outs of Nin's *Little Birds* before ordering pizza, an act which made Alice think of the evenings with her husband and kids in the now sold row-house, driving her deep into one of the bare corners of the freshly-painted white-walled rented bedroom to cry. '*Hey hey*,' said Louise crouching down to try and comfort her, 'it's going to be all right, you'll see. It's just going to take time to get used to all this.'

In retrospect, the Writing Centre had been the gateway job. As a part of her three-month (possibly renewable after reapplication and a lengthy in-person interview process) contract, Alice had to write 250 words after each student appointment. These 'reflection and measurable outcomes notes' as they were called, outlined the trajectory of the 45 min appointment in such a way as to describe the student/client's problems and the ensuing appointment results. As Alice had mentioned to one of her friends at the time, it was kind of therapy-based – how they were feeling, what they were anxious about, what were the next action-based steps they could take toward resolving their dilemmas – but it was also one step and 250 to 500 words away from an actual completed assignment that paid cold hard cash with no need to humiliate yourself every three months for eternity. Instead, you could write, get paid, and be guaranteed decent job security. This was so much more than any 21st-century university or college could offer. Sometimes, the students even thanked you. They were appreciative of your effort, for the time and work it took to write their essays for them. And tight deadlines were compensated extra as opposed to being regularly imposed as universities often hired instructors a mere week before the beginning of a course so that the conditions of work would deliberately be that of duress, fear and uncertainty.

Alice still often recalls that woman in one of her graduate seminars in Women's Studies at the Faculty of Education. She was quite beautiful with lush dark brown curls and often wore 1970s, early 1980s-style clothes. She carried herself in a determined, confident way and said she had worked as a high-school teacher for years before coming back to do her PhD in Education. She was concerned about teacher burnout and, specifically, about their soft and hard drug use which she claimed was absolutely rampant and of proportions that were positively epidemic. But at the time, no one really believed her as she had that wild look in her eye. Just like the guy who regularly carried around a big sign on a stick that outlined all the various grievances and wrongs that he personally had witnessed committed by the university. Most days he simply walked around with it, other days he might begin to profess and read off the list aloud to passers-by heading to class on campus. He and his wife, he said, had once been graduate students too. '*Beware!* You have only to read here about the hell you're heading into!'

So naturally, the woman's claims of drug-addicted teachers as a new social norm simply went unheeded.

Louise had stopped using for a while. She'd had a serious scare, and even flat-lined before being revived. Afterwards she'd joked about it. 'It's like the old Grace Slick quote about trips and roulette: sometimes it stops on "had a great time," another on "called my mother and cried," another "fell asleep early," another, "overdose and die." Ha! That Grace Slick, she's really got it down.' When Louise really did overdose and die, Alice was sure it was because of the work she'd been sent to do in the prisons. It was some new Women's Studies program, as if putting people on permanent contract weren't enough. Now they were being sent out to prisons in the name of social justice, as if the lowliest of the lowliest in the academic ranks should now be responsible for curing all of society's structural ills. Meanwhile, the latest yearly salary figures for a nearby university president (some sort of business or tax lawyer as so many administrators these days of course were) was over one million dollars! 'See if he'll go into the prisons in the name of education or social justice. I think not!' Alice used to say. That's the exact reason why she finally stopped taking contracts in Women's Studies in particular. The hypocrisy of lecturing on the need for social justice while being chronically exploited herself became too much to bear. And later, when her middle child entered university to study global sustainability but suddenly became suicidally depressed because our global crisis is, well, let's just say beyond the point of no return, Alice decided that she was simply tired of helping the universities rip students off.

At Louise's funeral, everyone made a big to-do. The head of Women's Studies made it her personal mission to ruin the Catholic mass in the name of feminism. After several proclamations publicly announcing Louise's sexual orientation at the pulpit, she began to solicit donations for a fund in Louise's name who had apparently now become the very face of the program itself. Students sobbed, TAs that Louise couldn't stand all gathered around holding one another in their collective yet turn-taking public display of grief. Some comforted the girlfriend who had failed to wake up because she was too drunk. Louise's mother, herself too once a teacher until she had to retire early due to chronic all-over bodily pain (hence the abundance and availability of used fentanyl patches for Louise), sat holding the ashes of her only daughter in the front row. Alice leafed through the photo albums that had been lain out around the room together with some of Louise's books – Willa Cather's O Pioneers! and, one of their collective favourites from a grad course in women's writing, also by Cather, My Ántonia. The vulgarity of the institution's logo on Louise's souvenir funeral card passed for collegiality, serving to both brand and turn the tragedy to their own purposes. Overdose? What overdose? the funeral card said. This is simply a life cut short, the face of Women's Studies fallen in the line of duty as she fought to make the promise of social equality a reality. The head of Women's Studies even went around saying it verbally, as if Louise hadn't been regularly walking around her apartment half-naked at night before her 8:30 a.m. class with a 280-student enrolment chewing and sucking on a used fentanyl patch.

The card was photocopied and put up on the bulletin board in between an advertisement for some new course purportedly combining anti-capitalist and environmentalist struggles and an announcement that a new slew of therapy animals would be available for petting and stroking between the hours of 10 a.m. and 2:30 p.m., weekends included. Some empty plastic water bottles were squashed down so they could be stapled as a border around the ad for the class, photos of dogs, cats, and even rabbits helped to announce the new hours for their petting availability in the new student center whose corporate sponsor was a subsidiary of one of the biggest multinationals producing bottled water. *If you go chasing rabbits, And you know you're going to fall, Tell them a hookah-smoking caterpillar has given you the call, Call Alice, when she's ten feet tall!* That Grace Slick, she's really got it down!

While people clucked and cooed to one another for months in front of the bulletin board, repeating the version of the tragedy they'd been fed under the eyes of the cameras installed in every nook and cranny of the institution in the name of student safety, no one noticed that Louise was stoned. They didn't see her high or realise that her glaze-eyed grin in the funeral/marketing photo had nothing remotely to do with social justice or the like. Instead, it had everything to do with residing in that little bit of space carved out to comfortably bear the weight of your fate of having been completely and repeatedly fucked over. *When the men on the chessboard get up and tell you where to go, And you've just had some kind of mushroom and your mind is moving low, Go ask Alice, I think she'll know! When logic and proportion have fallen sloppy dead, And the White Knight is talking backwards and the Red Queen's off with her head. Remember! What the dormouse said – Feed your head! Feed your head!* Alice just hoped the institution stopped there and didn't build some kind of statue of Louise out in one of the new courtyards with '*Trees by* (fill in the blank bank).'

Louise's girlfriend paid off the last of Louise's government student debt with the life insurance money she got before finally deciding it best just to leave town. Alice inherited a copy of Anaïs Nin's most quotable quotes with her famous '*To Lie, of course, is to engender insanity*' appropriately on the front cover, along with a score of *West Side Story* from way way back before any thought or talk of graduate school when Louise would break out into song as she prepared for her career on Broadway. And as Alice wrote yet another student essay, looking at Louise's funeral card permanently placed on top of her desk, she would imagine Louise singing her heart out on some Broadway stage instead of smiling out at her from the other side of her obituary like the Cheshire Cat.

AT THE RESALE SHOP

WELL, DID I TELL YOU yet 'bout when we went down on Ottawa Street? We went into the Resale Shop and lo and behold, there hanging in with all the other clothes was my orange dress! I couldn't believe it! It was the one Cheryl gave me.

So, I said to Wanda, 'what's my orange dress doing there? No wonder I couldn't find it!' And she said that they went through my stuff and took some of it to the Resale Shop. And I said, '*What!?* Without even asking me? That dress was a souvenir – I only wore it twice!' Cheryl bought it for me the year she got sick. We were out somewheres and I saw it and I said, 'oh what a pretty dress!' and that was the end a the conversation. Well, not a few days later she shows up at my house with the dress and I said, 'Oh Cheryl, you didn't have to spend your money like that.' And there it was on a rack in the Resale Shop on Ottawa Street. Mixed in with all the others!

Wanda said I should buy it back. And I said, 'Wanda, why would I buy my own dress back that I never even sold? *You* buy it back for me! And where did the money go for all those things anyway? I certainly didn't see none of it!' A course she never bothered to answer. Just kept on insisting that I had too much stuff and didn't wear a lot of it anymore.

'How would you know?' I said. 'I go to church! And besides,' I said to her, 'I wasn't dead, I was just moving. I understand about downsizing but how would you like it if I came in and went through all your things without you knowing it!' I had a nice white jacket with a kind of ruffle at the sleeve, it was a nice satiny material – I used to wear it a lot. I don't dare go to church with bare arms and that jacket was perfect.

That's terrible when people do that to you when you're old. All of it gone. Can you imagine your own kids doing that to you? Some skirts I didn't mind because I don't really wear that anymore, my legs are so ugly and full a veins, but the blouses and jackets – I had some real nice things and they belonged to me! And the orange dress Cheryl gave me. That was a keepsake, from *her*!

And my knitting books.

June wants me to knit a baby blanket. She says that all the kids have a blanket from Great Gramma. I really didn't have no intention of doing any more knitting because it really gives me a headache. But she said that all the kids have one so this one coming would be left out.

Well, I went to see what patterns I got and you know what? All my books are gone! They got rid a them when

I moved. All my patterns I had for years and years. You can't get them anymore. Without even asking!

Wanda said, 'Mom, you said you weren't going to be doing anymore knitting.'

'Well, I thought you kids were done having babies!'

But they're not. And just because Wanda's kids aren't having anymore kids doesn't mean that the others won't. I know Rita wants another and Lynn's havin' this one. How am I supposed to be doing any knitting without my patterns! All at the Resale Shop!

She said the Resale Shop for that is somewheres down on Tecumseh Road and that I could buy some a them back. Now I gotta spend money on my own patterns. I was so mad! They shoulda asked me. That was my decision not theirs. When I talk to her tomorrow I'm gonna ask her for the address. Though it won't do me no good anyways. I'm not going to be spending money on buyin' my own books back. What a waste.

Then, I heard them talkin'. Right now, I got the apartment with two bedrooms but they were saying that I could go down to just one and save some money on the rent. I said, 'Yeah? That's a good idea but I don't want to move.' They said, 'Oh don't worry, we'll move ya!'

And I said, 'thanks, but no! I want to hold onto the little things I got left now.'

DRINKING IN PUBLIC

'THE POLICE HAVE ARRIVED,' Seamus says, matter-of-factly. 'I'll have to call you back.'

'The police! What do you mean? What happened? What did you do?'

'I'll have to call you back,' he repeats.

'But what's going on? What did you do? *Please, tell me what you did!*'

'I'll call you back.'

'But what's going on?'

'Nothing. Nothing's going on. I'm drinking in public. I'll phone you later. Bye.'

And he hangs up the phone as if it's a matter of course that the police come right about now and arrest him. Nothing out of the ordinary or particularly *egregious*, as he would say. Just drinking in public and banging the receiver of the payphone several times against its base. I remember the first time he did it: the time when I told him that I didn't want to speak to him anymore when he was drunk. His voice was calm, even on the other end of the line. He wasn't upset, yelling or crying or even repeating himself, mouthing a string of words that he himself did not hear anymore and which I had stopped listening to several months before. His words were simple and well-paced, as if he were trying to have a conversation. Then, suddenly, five loud bangs, the smashing of two hard objects together.

'What was that? What's going on over there?'

'Nothing, nothing's going on.'

'Well, something's going on, I heard it.'

'*Oh? You heard it, Maude?* Long even pause. 'So does that mean you wanna hear it again? *Maude?* OK. Here it is again.' His voice is steady, smooth, unemotional. He smashes the phone against its base only twice this time before hanging up, and me, still there on the other end, just beginning to understand that I should be afraid. I put my cordless phone back in its cradle on top of the TV table, telling that part of me that is curious about where he is, what he might be doing and if he is allright, that I will not be running out to get him. I will not be going down somewhere on Yonge Street to pay a tab, and I will definitely not go down to the police station if he calls for me to pick him up. And I cannot, I insist to myself, go to the hospital to comfort him if he gets beat up.

It's the false sense of control that keeps you addicted to answering his ten to fifteen calls if it's a particularly bad day. The sense that while he's in the alcohol swirl, you're not, you're out and your life is OK. Everything is in order, or at least relatively manageable. He is slurring his words about kissing your belly and you're at work getting something accomplished. The phone helps to produce a distance, a feeling of comfort and control. The alcohol is in his apartment, not yours, and it is clearly he who is melting into a drunken crying mess on the floor. You could go over there anytime as he asked you to and feel superior. 'I don't know what exactly I can do, but sure, I'll come over at about seven.' You envision cleaning up his small apartment, throwing bottles away like you used to do when he was living in yours. You envision sweeping up, getting things in order, wiping away the booze stench with your grapefruit-scented cleanser. This is what you used to do time and time again, while lecturing him about his behavior. And then he would promise to try harder and swear his love and allegiance to you.

But what you didn't talk about was how the bottles moved from under the sink to deep in your bottom drawer to a plastic bag in the closet so he wouldn't find them and drink them when you weren't there. You don't talk about how that affected you. You didn't say anything about your relationship to their soothing content. Even now that you've come to pour them down the drain – *glug glug they took so long to empty* – and wash the sink out with the lemon smell of Mr Clean, even now that they're gone along with your little glass pipe for smoking, its pretty blue colour mixed with shades of red, yellow and green, you still don't say what these things mean to you.

He is sounding far too good. His voice even, steady, every-day there on the other end of the line. This means that he is on the upward trajectory of his high. His sober high that will reach an apex via his self-imposed stress followed then by the free and liberating alcohol high laced with depression so deep and severe that it becomes a hole.

I used to think that this was him. That this was Seamus. This tiny little phase of the cycle when he starts being able to carry a bit of the world on his shoulders, step into the details of the everyday. A street with people on it coming and going from work, stepping in line to buy a cup of coffee. Picking up dry cleaning with the clear transparent cello-phane bags. The sun shining. I used to hear this bit of con-fidence, control, this movement forward, gaining his stride, hear his open laugh and I would think: this is him. And eventually, this is the thing that will not only stretch out longer, ideally for the rest of our lives, but that will also become stronger and more developed until he is the loving, caring person that I know he is, *under all that*. But now, almost one year later, this everyday voice of his strikes terror and not hope in my chest and I fear that I can't bear the pain anymore.

An excruciating headache is what I've had all day, a pain that alternates from my left eye to my right. The everyday voice is, unlike what I once thought, a very, very bad sign. There is nothing hopeful about it. It predicts doom.

'But it's you who wears the pants, not me. I'm perfectly content to be the wife,' says Seamus. 'I mean, how hard can it be, cleaning the bathroom and cooking? I'll go down to Kensington to do the shopping. Peppers are three for a dollar there, not like those capitalist swine across the street where you go to at the Value Mart. And Jamaican patties. If you don't like those, you should. Montreal bagels, *mmm*. Do you remember when we went for coffee that very first time? I'd just come back from the market before heading over to the library. I'm glad you asked me too because I would have never asked you.'

'Why not?'

'Because. I'd never dare lift my head up that far. I might bump it on the underside of a table.'

And everything is fine until he needs a drink. This could be a period of two weeks, two months, or two days – it all depends. The people sitting at the next table drinking a beer while he's having a coffee, the smell of a bar filtering out its summertime patio from across the street as we walk along the south side of Bloor.

There are chips in my door and greasy fingerprints where he has tried to get in. I wipe them off with the lemon Mr Clean, trying to figure out when it was that he could have been here. He's left big gouges where he has kicked and scraped at the door, and there are punctures at hand level where perhaps a key held like a knife has been dug in. Why none of this particularly affects me, I don't really know. It should be frightening that he has done this to my door. I should be upset, crying or calling someone for help. Maybe I should call his sister again, although everyone in his family gives me the same old story. We all wish we could do something, but to do something, Seamus has to be receptive. And he isn't.

Thanks, for nothing.

The phone rings. I pick up. His mood is not repentant and he doesn't feel like being sad. 'So, do you want to know how I do this or what?' he asks, on the verge of getting very angry, yelling, perhaps ready to rap the receiver several times against the phone, table. 'If I tell you you're not going to hang up. You're fucking not going to hang up. DON'T YOU EVER HANG UP ON ME AGAIN!'

I am silent, listening on the other end.

'If you,' and here his tone softens slightly, he pauses and slows everything down to a kind of slouch and slur, 'if you want to spend the rest of your life with me because I sure as hell know I want to spend the rest of my life with you, you won't hang up on me again!'

'Go ahead, tell me,' I say, sitting there alone in the dark of my apartment, eyes heavy hurting because they see nothing but the back-and-forth muddled mess of the binge, the two of us alone in its depth, me dragged in, struggling to find some way out of his confusion becoming more and more violent. 'Tell me.'

'OK, OK,' he says. 'I'll tell you how this addiction thing works.'

I think his pauses are swigs of beer out of the slender neck of a Corona, 'are you drinking?'

'*What?*'

'Are you drinking? There's no use in lying.'

'There's no use in lying,' he repeats, mimicking me, and then laughs.

I don't really care if he's drinking or not, at this point.

I just want to know if I've correctly identified the nature of his pauses.

'I have a nice face,' he says. 'I do. I have a nice face. This is true. Don't you think? I have a nice face.'

'So?'

'So? I have a nice face and I'm a nice guy. And it's very easy for me to go up to someone and say "hey hi, how you doing" and then have a few drinks with them. Maybe one, maybe two, maybe more.'

'And then what?' His speech is slow but I can feel the violence in his voice, sitting there waiting, ready to come into his hands and fists. 'And then what?'

He pauses.

'Well, that's the thing. You never know. You never really know what exactly's going to happen.'

'But how do you get the cash to drink?' I prompt him, wanting him to admit it, confirm my suspicions about him, but he won't. He just goes off, starts to yell, insists that he's telling me, he's telling me how he does it. He's shouting, 'I TOLD YOU! I HAVE A NICE FACE!'

There are gaps, pauses, and the conversation breaks off into incomprehensibility interlaced with shouts, falling on the floor, banging of the phone, crying and burps.

'Are you telling me that you just go up to someone and start a conversation and start drinking with them?'

'Look, I'll tell you how this manipulation thing works.'

Silence, he has trailed off. And then, 'You can probably get two, two to three beers.'

'From who?'

'FROM THE BARMAN!' he shouts. He's angry, like he could pummel my head, crush it under his fist or with a bat.

I tell him that I don't want to know about this anymore and that if he comes around here or tries to call, I will phone the police.

His voice is pathetic. That is why you meet him even though you said said you wouldn't. You were just thinking how happy you are to be free from him for once when the phone rang and you decided to pick up. Why did you decide that? Because you know he'd be pathetic. You knew he'd be sorry and ready to cry. And he does. He is very, very sad.

'Please can you meet me? Please, can we hook up? I'm waiting for you to be finished work. Please say yes, you'll meet me.'

And I do. I say I'll meet him in one hour when the library closes, and even though I know he'll be drunk and looking a mess, maybe even drinking a can of beer and talking to himself so everyone can see, I say yes because I feel sorry for him. I feel sorry for his sadness, even though I almost understand there is nothing I can do. The best anyone can do is to take him home and hope that he takes the opportunity to sleep it off.

But when I show up to where he's waiting for me outside the library, he's not regretful or remorseful as he was on the phone. Instead there's some scufuffle at the hotdog stand. He has ordered a hotdog for which he cannot pay. He is hungry, he says.

His apartment keys are on a black shoe string tied around his neck. He doesn't feel like crying anymore, he's fine. Slight swagger and sway.

'Can I walk you home?'

He walks alongside me now trying to touch my face and brush back my hair all the while squinting one eye shut so he can focus. He's wearing a vivid aqua-coloured sweatshirt, the same colour as his eyes, one that I've never seen before. Where did he get it? We continue to walk until he stops, suddenly, holding his chest.

'What? What is it?'

'Nothing. Just go. Keep going!' And he shoos me away with his hand.

'What is it?'

'Just go!'

'Seamus, what's wrong?'

A crowd of students pass us by until we are alone, standing there in the middle of the sidewalk.

'OK!' He suddenly starts to raise his voice since the group has passed. 'I just felt like I was going to vomit. Is that OK, Maude, if I vomit? *Why does everything always have to be about you?*'

A HOUSE OF CARDS

IN THE OLDEN DAYS, children used to take their mothers in. Not like today; nobody wants them. But I'd better not squawk too much 'cause they're already getting ready to put me away. It's my legs lately that aren't doing so hot. But the reason for that is 'cause I haven't been walking. Usually, I walk the halls of my building. So that kinda leaves me on my own.

It's scary sometimes.

I remember calling up Seamus from Ridgetown. I was lying in the back bedroom of the single-width trailer after taking three Lorazepam. The phone had been ringing. A nurse was begging for someone to drive back to the hospital to sit with my mother. She was screaming, the nurse said. Trying to rip out all her tubes and shouting that the Gestapo was coming: 'They're coming to get me! Take me away for good – don't you people care?'

'I do care, I do care,' I'd said repeatedly to the nurse. 'It's just that I'm in no condition to drive. I can't drive right now. I can't stand up. I'm going to come in the morning. First thing.'

'What about your mother's husband? Can't he come?' she'd pleaded, along with the new nurse who'd come on for the next shift. Shut off in the little trailer bedroom, I lay listening to the sounds of people's garbled speech, his drunken laughter mixed in with the others in the next room. 'No,' I hear myself say to her, 'he can't come either. Please,' I begin to plead now, 'let me come in the morning. I'll be able to drive there then.'

That's when I called Seamus.

'*Seamus, please help me!* I've got to move when I come back to Toronto. I've got to get out of my apartment – please help me do that!'

'Of course, I'll help you if that's what you want. But Maude, you're just feeling like you need to resolve something. That's why you want to move. Just calm down. I'm here. I'm going to help you when you get back, don't worry. Allright?'

'Allright,' I say, putting the receiver of the old phone in the cradle on top of the multicoloured doily crocheted by someone in the park and sold for twenty-five cents at the Christmas-in-July community centre party. *Allright.*

Little Joe from Kokomo
Jimmi Hicks from the Sticks
Boxcars or Midnight
Little Phoebe and Snake Eyes

All those funny names to describe a toss of the dice. But they weren't so funny then. I don't know how many times we come home to find something else missin' after he'd lost a bet. One time he even took the stamp collection your mother always hid under the bed (*poor baby*) to pay off a debt. Another time it was the couch, and yet another the car. A bad throw of the dice and there we were – all of us paying for it. But honey, it's like I said: they don't pick their days! If they did, we coulda planned around them somehow, avoided them, especially when the kids were small and still looking to go at least for the day some-wheres, *all together*.

Like that one time we were set to go to Boblo Island. We wanted to have a picnic, to go on the rides at the amuse-ment park. Only instead a doing what was promised, he comes stumbling up the steps all whiskied up. But I said: 'Pile in the car kids! We're going to the island anyway!'

Next door, Flo was outside with her kids too and asked, 'Where are you all goin'?'

'Florence, I'm taking everyone to Boblo Island,' I told her. Then her kids started crying, 'we wanna go too! We wanna go too!'

'Well, I don't mind if you wanna take them too with you, Ruby.'

So, there I was, me and seven kids. It took a lot to chase after them all day long, but I was tired of Wally always disappointing them. Only when it was time to go, I was too late for the boat. I couldn't get all those kids to the dock on time so we had to wait for the next boat that was leaving for Windsor at 11 p.m. I guess by that time, your grandfather was starting in his drunken way to worry, and he called up Customs. He said, 'My wife's out with seven kids and I'm really worried. I don't know what happened to them all, it's nearly eleven o'clock!' So all the guys were there in their uniforms looking for me, and when we finally got to Customs, the attendant said, 'Are you the lady with seven kids? Your husband Walter keeps calling here and he's worried sick!'

'He is?' I said. '*Since when!*'

I'm pretty sure it was him though, who was coming to your mother. She said she kept seeing a man in her room, real late at night. Poor darlin' musta been so scared to stay alone there at the hospital. I know I would be. She said that one time a man popped right up out of the umbrella stand they had there in the corner of the room. Other times, he'd just be sitting in that blue reclining chair they had for visitors. 'Waiting and watching, looking out the window,' she said, 'straight across Tecumseh Road.' Yep, that was Wally allright. Trying to make up for all the things past I guess, come to finally comfort her. Make it so she wouldn't be so scared to die. 'Cause in the end, each one of us is alone.

§

'Maude, you've got to be *sovereign!*' Seamus would say to me both drunk and sober. 'I can't always be standing here waiting with my catcher's mitt.' The Christmas-in-July doily now sits in my new apartment, on top of a low wooden bookshelf I bought second-hand. 'That's what life is like with an alcoholic,' I hear Gramma Ruby say in my mind's ear – *nothin' but a house of cards.* You build something up, only to have it all come tumbling down without so much as a moment's notice. Like those little wooden penny dolls they used to have for kids. Push in the string at the bottom and they just fold right up, collapsing in on themselves.

The last time I saw Seamus was somewhere in the depths of downtown, streets grimy with the summer heat. He said he was going to hit me up for some money and that the coffee's on me. Instead, I bought him lunch plus cigarettes. 'You look nice today,' I said, which was true. A button-down short-sleeve shirt, and pants. It's not till I'm sitting close though that I notice stains down the front with food and booze and other things that don't bear thinking upon. By the time he takes his last drag of his second cigarette, he's already into the mood I know so well of getting antsy for another drink.

§

We'd argued more than once about her funeral. 'What do you mean you're not comin' to my funeral?' Gramma Ruby had said.

'Funerals are for the living,' I'd replied. 'Aren't they? And besides, there'd only be a big fight between everybody. Look at what happened with my mother. Is that what you want to happen at yours?'

'No, no. I suppose not. I know that John's not goin' to be flying in for it, that's for sure. The rest of them will just tear him to shreds. Lucy and Wanda, nothing but oil and vinegar. And Carl and Joe? Well, that'll be just like fireworks!'

I hear Gramma Ruby, her thoughts, judgements, memories a permanent voice in my head. Calling out to me in the same way the river calls out to me once I'm alone, moved far away with kids all grown. Where there are no more of my kin or kind, hands turning into old woman, stiff in the morning and somehow thicker. Reminding me of my mother's hands when I was a child, still wanting and trailing after her as she stretched out her arms and beckoned me, *'hurry up and come along!'* The Detroit River calling from its one hundred and eighty-six-foot depths, the cut straight and narrow, just as deep at the sides as in the middle. No shore, no gradual decline, the water deep and just as dangerous at the edge.

Like walking off a cliff.

ACKNOWLEDGEMENTS

Stories from this book have appeared in the following publications: *The New Quarterly, ELQ: Exile Literary Quarterly, The Windsor Review, Riddle Fence, Joyland,* and *This Will Only Take a Minute: 100 Canadian Flashes* (Guernica Editions, 2022).

I am grateful for the financial support received from the Canada Council for the Arts, the Ontario Arts Council, and from the Banff Centre for Arts and Creativity.

 **MUNKEN**

Learn more about the paper we use:

www.arcticpaper.com

Arctic Paper UK Ltd
8 St Thomas Street
London
SE1 9RS